BLACKOUT

BLACKOUT

Betty Sullivan La Pierre

www.SYNERGEBOOKS.COM

Cover Designs by Author, Paul Musgrove

This novel is a work of fiction. The characters, names, incidents, dialogue, and plot are the products of the author's imagination or are used fictitiously. Any resemblance to actual person, companies, or events is purely coincidental.

ISBN 1-59109-795-9

BLACKOUT

Others in "The Hawkman Series" by
BETTY SULLIVAN LA PIERRE
http://www.geocities.com/e_pub_2000

THE ENEMY STALKS
DOUBLE TROUBLE
THE SILENT SCREAM
DIRTY DIAMONDS

Also by Betty Sullivan La Pierre

MURDER.COM
THE DEADLY THORN

www.SYNERGEBOOKS.COM

The author wished to acknowledge the invaluable assistance and encouragement of the following establishment and members:
SANTA CLARA SPORTING CLUB BINGO
Agostinho S. Marques, Debbie Sadler, Dixie Waechter, Edgar Avila, Francisco Brasil, Lee Cox, Linda Avila, Luis Azevedo, Manuel Lourenco, Ralf Cebrian, Ray Waechter, Sebastiao Goncalves, Tarcisio Brasil.

To the memory of
Jim Gray

CHAPTER ONE

Hawkman shut down the computer, stretched his arms above his head then twisted his shoulders back and forth. Sitting in front of the monitor for hours at his office on a Sunday afternoon made him feel stiff all over.

His gaze shifted to the entry. He could have sworn he heard a soft knock. Tilting his head, he listened. Sure enough, it sounded again. He didn't have any appointment scheduled for today, so who could this be?

Crossing the room, he grabbed the handle and threw open the door. He peered down at a small black child about five or six years old. Her big brown eyes twinkled under a mass of ebony ringlets framing her face. Clutching a rag doll in her arms, she stared up at him with a big smile exposing several gaps in her front teeth. "You must be Mr. Hawk Man. Grandpa said you had a boo boo on your eye."

He stifled a grin and dropped to his haunches. "That's right. What's your name and what can I do for you?"

"I'm Amanda." Then she turned and pointed down the stairs. "My Grandpa wants to talk to you, but he can't get up here."

"I guess I better go down there then," Hawkman said, closing the door behind him and following the little girl.

She led him alongside the parking lot toward a large oak tree where a man as black as coal dust sat in a rickety wheelchair protected by the shade. Tufts of curly white hair stuck out from underneath his worn leather cowboy hat. He glanced up and grinned, holding out his hand as they approached. "Hawkman, you son of a gun, how come you don't get no older?"

Hawkman grabbed the man's hand with both of his. "Jesse, you old buzzard, where've you been keeping yourself? Haven't seen you in ages. It's good to see ya." He then turned and patted the little girl's shoulder. "How'd you come by such a pretty little granddaughter?"

The old man shoved his hat back and scratched his head. Eyeing the little girl, he pushed his fingers into one of the bib pockets of his overalls and pulled out a couple of dollars. He pointed toward one of the stores next to Hawkman's office. "Amanda, see that little shop over there?"

Her eyes glistening with anticipation, she whirled around and vigorously nodded. "Yes, sir."

"You go do a little shopping. Take your time, but don't talk to no strangers and come straight back here when you're through."

"Okay, Grandpa. I promise I'll be real careful." Grinning, she plopped her rag doll into his lap and grasped the bills in her fist.

Jesse watched the child dash across the lot and disappear inside the store. Then he turned his focus back on Hawkman. "I'm concerned about my daughter."

"Is that Destiny's little girl?" Hawkman asked, rubbing the back of his neck. "Somehow, I can't picture her being old enough to have a family."

The old man moved the doll from his lap and propped it up beside him. "Yep, that's Destiny's baby. I didn't know what to do with a female child after my Rose died. 'Fraid I let the girl run wild. She got mixed up with the wrong crowd and ended up pregnant. At least she had enough scruples not to have an abortion, but she flat refused to give the child up for adoption. Said it was hers and she'd raise it. Well, I couldn't argue with that, so she's been with me ever since. Fortunately, she shaped up. She's a fine mother and got a good job."

"So what's the problem?" Hawkman asked.

"Everything was going okay until two nights ago." He looked away.

"Yeah, go on."

"She never came home from playing bingo."

"Has she stayed out the whole weekend before?"

The old man shook his head. "Destiny's never done anything like this. She'd even call me when she had to drop by the grocery store on the way home from the office. Her guilt about me having to watch Amanda while she worked, made her very caring, especially after I got hurt and ended up in this danged wheelchair." He slapped the hand rests in disgust.

"Sorry about that, Jesse. How'd it happen?"

He waved a hand in the air. "Tell you about it another time. Right now, I need your help in finding Destiny."

Hawkman leaned against the trunk of the tree. "Okay, clue me in on the events before she left the house."

"Destiny never went out and had fun. I didn't think it healthy for a pretty young woman to stay home all the time. So last week I told her she needed to get out with her friends. I'd take care of Amanda. She called me Friday at her lunch break and told me she'd decided to go play bingo with Rene. They'd grab a bite to eat beforehand, then head over to the hall. She figured she'd be home by eleven or so. That's the last time I talked to her." The old man pulled a handkerchief from his pocket, blew his nose and wiped a tear from his eye.

"Have you talked to her friend?" Hawkman asked.

Jesse shoved the hanky back into the bib pouch in his overalls and nodded. "Yeah. When Destiny didn't show by noon on Saturday, I gave Rene a call."

"What'd she say?"

He sighed. "She told me Destiny won a bunch of money and decided since she was on a roll, she'd head for one of the Indian Casinos, thinking maybe she could make a bigger killing. Rene couldn't go with her as she had an appointment Saturday morning, so they parted ways outside the bingo hall. That was the last Rene heard from her. Now, she's concerned, as sometimes low life types hang out in those places."

"I've heard they have pretty good security in the casinos," Hawkman said.

"That's not what worries me. I'm afraid if anyone followed

Destiny from the bingo hall after she won all that money, she might not have made it to the casino. She could be lying in a ditch some place with her throat slit." The old man choked back a sob. "And to think I encouraged her to go out for the evening."

Hawkman reached over and patted him on the arm. "Now, Jesse, don't let your imagination run wild. She'll probably be home tonight with a good explanation."

"I'd like to believe that, Hawkman. But I'm really worried."

"Where is this bingo hall?"

The old man glanced up. "I don't have the vaguest idea."

Hawkman pulled a pad of paper and pen from his pocket and handed it to Jesse. "Write down the girlfriend's name and phone number. If Destiny doesn't show up tonight, I'll give the gal a call tomorrow and try to get more information." He wrote his cell phone number on the back of one of his business cards and gave it to Jesse. "Call me at this number in the morning and let me know one way or the other."

Jesse slid the card into his billfold and grimaced. "I'll have to pay you monthly."

Hawkman waved his hand. "We'll worry about that when we know you really need my services."

At that moment, Amanda came running up with a big smile and bright eyes. She held up her sack loaded with cheap toys. "I really got some good buys," she cried with glee.

Grandpa peeked into the bag. "Wow, you sure did." He glanced up and winked. "This little gal knows how to shop."

Hawkman left the two examining Amanda's purchases and headed back toward his office, his mind reeling with Jesse's story. He knew this man well enough that he wouldn't seek his help if he didn't think it necessary. Hawkman definitely didn't like what he'd heard so far. The smell of foul play worried him.

When Hawkman arrived home, his wife, Jennifer,

recognized the solemn expression of concern and handed him a beer. "What's up?"

"I'm hoping nothing, but I've got my doubts."

"Want to talk about it?"

Hawkman told her about Jesse's visit. "He's really aged, his hair is completely white, and on top of that, he's in a wheelchair."

"Oh, no! What happened?"

"He was so concerned about Destiny, he didn't elaborate, said he'd tell me another time. I saw him leave in his old pickup, so he can drive. His problem must stem from his back or his hips, making it difficult to walk."

Jennifer frowned. "I certainly don't like the idea of Destiny not returning home. It sounds like the girl has gotten her life straightened out, and her not contacting her dad sounds like trouble."

"Keep your fingers crossed that she comes home tonight. Jesse promised to call me in the morning."

Jennifer felt a shiver roll down her spine. "Who would take care of Amanda if something's happened to Destiny? A man of Jesse's age and condition couldn't be expected to raise that young child."

"Let's hope it doesn't come to that." Hawkman leaned forward on the kitchen bar. "You know anything about bingo?"

She shrugged. "A little. I've gone with some of my friends a few times. Why?"

"Can you win a lot of money?"

"Oh yeah, if you're lucky. One night I saw a gal win close to two thousand dollars."

Hawkman let out a whistle. "Just by winning one game?"

"Nowadays there's more to it than just bingo. They have flash boards, Cherry Bells, Keno and all sorts of odd games that can be played. Many are worth a thousand dollars at one whack."

He shot her a look. "You're kidding."

"No, I'm very serious. Also, they have bingo machines, sort of like mini-computers. You pay a bundle to play them.

The price depends on how many cards you want programmed into it. The more cards, the greater your odds of winning. All you have to do is punch in the numbers and the machine takes care of the rest. It's programmed for whatever game is on the menu."

He raised his brows. "Man, technology has come a long way in changing that game. I remember my Grandma talking about her church bingo. They used cardboard cards with bean markers and the prize would be a can of corn or a box of cereal. Then the last big payoff of the evening might be a Monopoly Board Game or something comparable.

Jennifer laughed. "Yes. I've heard those stories. But, the Indian Casinos have even bigger stakes, plus they have slot machines in the same building where the bingo games are held. It's a big operation now."

Hawkman drummed his fingers on the counter. "So, if Destiny won a bundle at bingo and someone noticed, she could have been followed . . . Jesse could be right. She might never have made it to the Indian Casino."

CHAPTER TWO

The next morning, Hawkman went to the aviary located on the outside deck and tended to his falcon's needs. Pretty Girl flapped her wings in recognition. "Tomorrow I'll take you for a hunt, girl. But today you'll have to be satisfied with man-made food." The bird squawked in protest.

After sweeping out the cage, he strolled into the kitchen and had just poured a cup of coffee when his cell phone rang. He almost dropped the mug, sloshing the liquid all over the counter surface as he yanked the instrument from his belt. "Hello."

"This is Jesse." His voice quivered. "Destiny didn't come home last night."

Hawkman sucked in a deep breath. "I'll get right to work. Will you be home today?'

"I ain't goin' nowhere."

"I'll be at your place within two to three hours. Meanwhile, I want you to call Detective Williams and file a missing person's report. He may tell you it's too soon, but you tell him Hawkman told you to."

"Okay," he said, coughing.

He figured the old man would use any means to cover his brimming emotions. "Jesse, we'll find her."

"Yeah, but how?" His tone flattened. "Dead or alive?"

Giving him a few moments, Hawkman cleared his throat. "Keep the prayers going. I'll see you soon."

"If anyone has hurt my Destiny, they'll have to deal with me."

Then the line went dead.

His gut aching, Hawkman clipped the phone back on his belt and envisioned Jesse in the wheelchair. His legs might be gone, but the massive shoulders, strong arms and hands were still there. He wouldn't want to be caught in one of Jesse's clutches. The man had lost his wife in a horrible accident and now his only child was missing. Right now, the thing keeping him sane was Amanda. He'd seen the love for that little girl in the old man's eyes.

Going over to the hanging coat rack that Jennifer had posted as 'Hawkman's Corner', he searched through his jacket pockets until he found the note with Rene's phone number. He grabbed a pencil, then picked up the portable phone on the kitchen counter and punched in the number.

"Rene Taylor, please".

"This is John, her husband, may I ask who's calling."

"Tom Casey, Private Investigator. I'd like to ask her some questions about Destiny Wilson."

"Hasn't she returned home yet?"

"No. I'm afraid not."

"Uh, oh, this doesn't sound good."

"Let's not jump to conclusions, Mr. Wilson. Is Rene there?"

"No, she's at work. Here's her number."

Hawkman jotted it down. "Thanks." He pushed the handset button then dialed.

"Barney & Baker Law Offices, Rene speaking. How may I help you?"

"Hello, Mrs. Taylor, my name's Tom Casey, Private Investigator."

"Oh, I know you. You're Hawkman," she chuckled. "A well known name around this law office."

He laughed. "Now I place you. I thought your name sounded familiar. Yes, I've had dealings with Barney & Baker. But I'm calling today to talk to you about Destiny Wilson. I promise not to tie you up for long."

"No problem. So what's with Destiny?"

"I understand that you and she went to bingo last Friday night."

"Yes, we did. Her daddy called me yesterday. Dear God, don't tell me she hasn't returned home yet?"

"Unfortunately, Jesse hasn't heard a word from her and he's very concerned. I need to know the name of the bingo hall that you ladies attended and what time you left."

"It's the White Oak Hall at the end of Main Street, and I'd say we got out of there close to ten thirty."

"Did Destiny indicate that she planned on going straight home?"

"No. She'd won fifteen hundred dollars at bingo, and decided to hit the Indian Casino to see if she could double her money. I wanted to go too, but had an early morning appointment. Damn, now I wish I'd skipped it and gone with her. I'm worried."

"Did you notice anyone paying special attention when she won? Or follow her out of the parking lot?"

"Oh, dear Lord, no, I didn't. My thoughts just didn't include anything dangerous as that's a pretty safe area."

"I understand. Did Destiny normally take off like this on her own?"

"Heavens, no. You couldn't get that girl to go anywhere at night. She felt so obligated to her daddy for taking care of Amanda during the day that she'd rush right home from work to fix dinner for the family and put the child to bed. But Friday night seemed special because her daddy insisted she take a night off and go have some fun." She sighed and grew silent for a moment. "Oh my, this must be tugging something terrible at Jesse's heart."

"Yes, it is, but hopefully we'll find Destiny unharmed. Thank you for your time and may I call you again if I have other questions?"

"Sure. Any time."

After hanging up, Hawkman took a deep breath and closed his notebook. He glanced up at Jennifer who'd just come into the kitchen.

"So Destiny didn't make it home last night?"

Hawkman shook his head.

Frowning, she sat down opposite him with her cup of coffee. "This doesn't look good."

"No. I don't like it at all." He shrugged into his jeans jacket, then lifted his hat from the coat rack shelf and plopped it on his head. "I don't know when I'll be home."

"I understand, but please keep me posted."

"I will," he said, pressing his lips softly to her forehead.

Hawkman left the house and climbed into his 4X4. He drove over the bridge and headed for Medford. When he reached town, he stopped at the police station and went straight to Detective Williams' office. Hawkman first peered around the door frame. All he could see was a mussed salt and pepper mane bent over a stack of papers. "Are they ever going to get you any help?"

The detective jerked up his head. "I figured you'd be by sometime today."

"Oh, yeah. Why's that?"

"I got a call from Jesse Wilson. He claims his daughter is missing."

Hawkman pulled up a chair and told him what he'd found out so far. "I don't like the way things are going down. She always kept in touch with her dad and he hasn't heard a word from her."

"Yeah, that's the picture I got. I did a quick check after he called and there haven't been any accidents or bodies found in the past seventy two hours. So we can rule that out so far. What's your take?"

"Don't like the way things are setting up. Just started my investigation and the trail seems to stop outside the bingo hall. Destiny won over a thousand dollars and I'm wondering if robbery might play a role?"

The detective nodded. "Very likely. Especially if someone kept track of the winners. They'd naturally go after the big stuff."

Hawkman scratched his sideburn. "Do you know anything

about bingo?" he asked sheepishly. "Is the hall open seven days a week?"

Williams grinned mischievously. "You thinking about taking up the game?"

CHAPTER THREE

Hawkman left the detective's office and headed out of town toward the Wilsons' farm. He remembered the first time he'd met Jesse and Rose. They'd come running into the emergency room at the same time he'd been rolled into the hospital after a sniper had put a hole in his leg. Jesse was carrying Destiny's limp body, tears streaming down his face. Rose ran by his side almost hysterical.

"Something's wrong with my baby girl. She's really hot and we can't get her to wake up," she cried frantically at the staff.

Hawkman vaguely remembered telling the doctors to take care of the child first.

The next day, Jesse visited Hawkman in the hospital, thanking him for his consideration. They'd been friends ever since.

He turned into the long driveway that led to a neat wood frame house. The brown bloodhound, turning gray around the eyes, lay on the front porch next to a rocking chair. He raised his head, let out a low howl, then dropped his nose back onto his paws. He thumped his tail a few times on the wooden planks when Hawkman jumped from his truck and strolled across the yard.

"Hey, Rochester."

The dog jumped up, obviously recognizing his voice, and let out several happy barks, then twitched his tail rapidly.

Hawkman hopped up the steps and petted his head. "Sorry I interrupted your nap. You can lie back down now."

Rochester settled back on his rug, but kept his soulful gaze on the tall man with the eye patch.

Jesse came to the door before Hawkman knocked, and pushed open the screen. He glanced down at the hound. "I can't get him to come inside. He's waiting for Destiny and has howled like he's in pain for the past two nights." Shaking his head, Jesse gestured with a wave of his hand. "Come on in."

Hawkman stepped inside to a cozy living room that smelled of roasted chicken and homemade bread. "Your house always smells good. It makes a man's stomach rumble."

"Can't cook as good as my Rose though," Jesse said, limping with the aid of his cane toward a straight-back chair next to the couch. He pointed at the sofa. "Have a seat."

Hawkman glanced around before sitting down. "Where's Amanda?"

"I don't want her here while we talk about her mama. One of the neighbors took her to go play in the park with her kids."

Hawkman nodded. "Good thinking. No sense in scaring her."

Jesse grumbled. "The child's only six, but she knows something's wrong. Her mama's never been away from her this long. She's asked me a million questions already. And hard ones, too."

"I can imagine," Hawkman said. "Well, we might as well get on with it. I need to know what kind of car Destiny drove that night."

Jesse reached over and removed a file from the top of the television. "I knew you'd need some of that stuff, so I collected it and put it in here." He handed the folder to Hawkman.

Thumbing through the papers, he glanced at the old man. "You did a good job. So she drives a green two door Ford Escort coupe?"

"Yep."

Hawkman jotted down the license number, then glanced at Jesse. "Do you remember what she wore that day?"

"Normally, I wouldn't have noticed. But she had on the royal blue pants outfit that I gave her for her birthday. Always thought she looked so pretty in it and remember telling her so that morning. She had a white blouse on under the jacket and a long silver-chained locket that has a picture of Amanda inside. She wears that with everything. I don't remember what kind of earrings she had on, but she always wears some."

"That helps a lot," Hawkman stated. "Do you have a fairly recent picture of her?"

He pointed at the file with his cane. "In the back. I stuck one in that shows her in that outfit."

Hawkman fingered through the papers. "Ah, here it is." He studied it for a moment, then glanced at Jesse. "Destiny certainly grew into a beautiful young woman. Can I keep this?"

"Oh, yeah. Anything in that file you need, you take it."

Leafing through the sheets, Hawkman frowned. "I don't see anything in here about Amanda's father. So, what's the story on him?"

Jesse sat with both hands resting atop his cane, his expression thoughtful as he stared at Hawkman. "You really need to know that?"

"Yes."

Sighing, Jesse leaned back in the chair letting the cane fall against his leg.

"His name is Roland Alexander, Jr."

Hawkman shot him a look.

"Yep, he's old man Alexander's son, but he doesn't know that his boy is the father of my granddaughter."

"That kid's been in all kinds of trouble. And his dad always knew about it and got him out of numerous scrapes. How'd he escape not knowing about Amanda?"

"Destiny didn't want anyone to know. She made me swear on the Bible never to tell. In fact, we don't even think the young man is aware that he has a daughter. You're the first person I've ever told and I want you to swear to keep it to yourself." Jesse reached over and took the old worn leather covered Bible from the arm of the sofa. "Put your hand on this here good book, Hawkman, and swear you won't tell a soul unless it's absolutely necessary."

"Glad you added that phrase, Hawkman said, gazing at

the man as he put his right hand on the Bible. "I swear to keep Amanda's daddy a secret, unless absolutely necessary."

Jesse nodded and put the manual back on the couch. "Thank you."

"How can you be sure Roland doesn't know? Kid's talk."

The old man grimaced as he ran his hand over the stubble on his chin. "Roland, who's a year older than Destiny, invited her to attend his graduation party at the school. She said a bunch of the kids went to the school celebration for awhile, but then decided to leave. Once they left the building, the authorities wouldn't let them back inside. So, they decided to throw their own bash. Somehow they snagged a bunch of liquor and went to the park where they got drunk out of their heads."

Hawkman rolled his eyes. "Teens drive you nuts and they wonder why we come down on them so hard."

"None of them was fit to drive, so at least they stayed put. Unfortunately, they turned on the car radio and the girls didn't have the sense to keep their clothes on. They started strip dancing and you can pretty well guess what happened. Destiny swears that Roland was the only boy who actually got to her, even though she heavy petted with a lot of the others. She swears he's the daddy."

"So she never approached him about it?"

Jesse shook his head. "Nope. I wanted her to get some DNA testing for Amanda's sake." He pointed a crooked finger in the air. "One of these days, that little girl is going to want to know who her daddy is. And not only that, he should be paying something for the raising of that child." His shoulders sagged. "But Destiny wouldn't hear of it. Said Roland's a slob, and she wanted nothing to do with him. It also frightened her that if the boy's daddy, with all his money, ever found out the child belonged to Roland, they might try to take her away. She couldn't stand the thought."

Hawkman leaned back on the sofa and remained silent for a few moments.

The old man frowned. "What's brewing in that head of yours? Not like you to be so quiet."

"Did Destiny hang around this area after she got pregnant? Did people know?"

Jesse shook his head. "I sent her back to Oklahoma to my sister's. Then when she came home, she made up the story that Amanda belonged to a cousin who was going to put the child up for adoption. Destiny boasted to her friends that she'd rescued the baby and brought her home to raise. I doubt anyone believed it, but no one disputed it either. Why do you ask?"

"Amanda's mulatto like the Alexanders. And the more I think about it, the child's facial features remind me of that family."

Jesse shivered. "I know. The older she gets, the more she looks like her daddy."

"Has Roland been around?"

The old man let out a long sigh, and nodded. "Yeah, just recently. He's called Destiny on the phone and even dropped by the house a couple of times. But my girl won't have a thing to do with him. She told me that Roland had divorced his wife of a year and is on the prowl."

"Has he taken much notice of Amanda?"

"Can't rightly say. Destiny doesn't invite him inside and if I bring up her bad manners, she has a fit. Tells me that the man isn't worthy of courtesy and his name is banned in our household."

"Why would she be so bitter, when it's as much her fault as his that she got pregnant?"

Jesse shrugged. "I've asked her the same thing, but she doesn't have much of an answer. I think she's ashamed. Yet, she loves Amanda more than life."

"I will more than likely have to question him at some time or another. But it will only be about Destiny. So don't be alarmed if you hear about me stopping at the Alexanders."

"I understand." His Adam's apple bobbed up and down as he fought his emotions.

Hawkman decided that was enough for now and changed the subject. "Tell me, Jesse, how'd you get all crippled up?"

"Damned horse threw me. One of my cows due to calve

didn't show up one evening with the rest of the herd. So I saddled my mare and went out huntin' for her. Horse got spooked over something and reared. Off I went. Landed on my back in a stack of rocks. Ain't been right ever since."

"Real sorry to hear that, Jesse. Is there anything the doctors can do?"

"Oh, I suppose they could operate, but don't want to take the chance they'll mess me up for good. Right now I can at least get around. I have a little pain, just can't walk too well."

Hawkman stood. "That's about all I need right now. This information will get me going. No need to see me to the door, but keep that file handy, and let me know immediately if you hear from Destiny."

Jesse nodded and wiped his eyes.

He stepped out onto the porch and Rochester let out a mournful howl. Hawkman reached down and stroked his head. "We'll find her, old boy."

CHAPTER FOUR

Hawkman left Wilson's and drove slowly by the neighboring Alexander ranch, studying the layout as he passed. His gut told him Roland might know something about Destiny. Word spread fast in this small rural community and it wouldn't be long before they all knew that she had disappeared. But he'd wait awhile. He needed more information before talking to the young man.

Detective Williams informed him that the White Oak Bingo Hall opened every night. Jennifer had explained that various organizations leased the building for different nights and some had contracted it for several evenings of the same week. She didn't know who ran it on Fridays. He'd just have to ask some questions to find out who and when. Jennifer also told him the doors usually opened around four in the afternoon for those who wanted to come early and take advantage of the snack bar before playing. He figured by the time he arrived, some of the staff would be there.

He parked in front of the building that displayed a large banner strung above the door with the word 'BINGO' in large red letters. Having always associated the game with ladies and senior citizens, it surprised him to see many were from the younger set and a great number of men were entering the establishment.

Hawkman strolled inside and stood by the front door surveying the two large rooms. One separated the other by a glass wall with the sign over a swinging door that stated; 'No-Smoking'. Rows of tables and chairs ran lengthwise across the floors, broken into sections by two aisles. Eight television monitors, two to a wall, were attached near the ceiling and faced inward toward the crowd. In between each of these were large boards with lighted numbers and on the end, a moving design displaying the bingo pattern to be played. An elevated stage area with a large desk-like podium supporting a computer system stood at the far end of the hall. Hawkman figured that space belonged to the caller.

Several people mingled around the tables, chatting and laughing. Soon, a short stocky man, his eyeglasses hanging off one ear and the rest of the frame floating under his chin, approached him. His eyes twinkled as he grinned mischievously. His balding head gleamed, except for a fringe of graying hair around the edges. In his hand, he held a stack of small colorful cards.

"Hello, you want some flash boards?" he asked with a Portuguese accent. "This is my favorite game." He held them in front of Hawkman's face.

"I don't even know what they are," he said laughingly and held out his hand. "My name's Tom Casey and I'm a private investigator. I'd like to speak to the manager."

The man quickly slipped on his glasses, shook his hand, then stared into Hawkman's face with a grimace. "What did you say you were?"

He took out his badge.

The man looked at the shiny piece of metal with wide eyes, then he frowned. "Oh, my. A private investigator. Are we in trouble?"

Hawkman grinned at the colorful character and shook his head. "I don't think so. I'm more interested in one of your customers."

"Uh, oh. You better come with me and talk to our head guy." He waved for him to follow. "Come on, come on," he said impatiently. "I have to get back to work, you know."

Hawkman trailed him to an area that appeared to be some sort of an office but looked like a booth with three open windows. Inside were two men, one bald, who very much resembled the person he followed. He appeared very busy passing out strange looking black machines and sets of papers with squares of numbers. Another gentleman stood near the back over a tall table sorting money. Hawkman glanced at the other open cubicle built alongside this one. People stood behind a counter collecting money and dealing out a variety of small cards similar to the ones the man had tried to sell him.

Hawkman stared in awe at the excitement and activity, when suddenly, a scream echoed from across the room. His gaze darted toward the sound and his hand automatically went to his holster. A woman danced around her chair in glee while holding up one of the cards. He couldn't imagine why until the man with the swinging glasses pointed.

"Oh my gosh, looks like she just won an instant."

"An instant what?" Hawkman asked, his hand dropping to his side.

The man rolled his eyes. "Two hundred and fifty dollars. Boy, you don't know anything about bingo, do you?"

Hawkman grinned and shook his head. "Not a thing."

"Hee, hee, hee," he chuckled. "Well, you just hang around here for a little while and you'll learn."

Finally, attracting the attention of the man handling the money, the funny seller motioned for him to come to the window. "I think we have a problem," he said in a low husky voice. He hooked a thumb toward Hawkman. "This guy's a private eye and he wants to talk to you." He then turned and headed out toward the center of the room, holding up the cards and bellowing, "Seasons, my favorite game."

The manager's smile turned to a frown as he glanced at Hawkman. "Is something wrong?"

"This has nothing to do with the operation of the bingo hall. I just need to know if this is the same group that runs the Friday night games."

"Yes," he said, with a questioning tone. "We lease the halls four nights a week, Monday, Tuesday, Friday and Saturday. Why?"

Hawkman pulled the picture of Destiny out of his pocket. "Do you remember seeing this woman last Friday?"

He studied the picture for a few moments. "I don't recognize her, but I'm usually not on the floor. You might ask some of the workers. Why the interest in this particular woman? Is she in some kind of trouble?"

"She hasn't been seen since she left this hall last Friday night."

The manager's thick eyebrows shot up as he raked a hand across his forehead, pushing back fallen hair strands. "You mean she just disappeared?"

"Yes. And from what I understand, she won a lot of money here that night."

"Oh my Lord," he swore in a whisper. "Just a moment."

He turned away from Hawkman, went out the rear door of the small office and came around to where he stood. "Let me get one of the workers and we'll go outside. It's too hard to speak privately in here. "I want you to show him that photo."

Waving at the man with the hanging glasses, he led the way outside and into the parking lot. The manager introduced the worker to Hawkman. "This is Argo Biton, we call him Argy. I'm Patrick Telephus, known as Teley, I run the place with everyone else's help ."

Hawkman shook hands with the two men, then presented the picture of Destiny to Argy. "Do you remember seeing this young woman last Friday night?"

He quickly slid on his glasses and stared at the snapshot. "She looks like the one who won a lot of money. But I'm not sure. Dolly or Ed will know, since they did the payouts.

"Are they here tonight?" Hawkman asked.

Argy glanced at Teley and shrugged.

"Ed just left on an errand and will be back shortly. I expect Dolly any moment."

"Mind if I wait?"

Teley shook his head. "Not at all. Come on inside and sit at one of the tables. As soon as either of them shows up, I'll introduce you."

"Thanks. Appreciate it."

Hawkman sauntered over to the snack bar where he

ordered a hot dog and soda. Seeking out an empty table near the door, he sat down and returned the stares of the patrons. As he munched, his attention turned to the entry when he heard, "Hi Dolly".

A woman not much over five feet tall with collar length shiny blond hair strolled into the room. Her smile and sparkling blue eyes lit up the area. Wearing a cotton blouse rolled up at the sleeves, with its tails hanging on the outside of her blue jeans, she walked in with a confident air that signified she knew all about this place. She went to the office cubicle and stuck her head inside the open window. The manager immediately called her inside. Hawkman could see them talking and sensed the discreetness Teley used as he spoke to her. When he turned and pointed toward Hawkman, she nodded, exited the door and crossed the floor toward his table.

As she approached, she held out her hand. "Hi, I'm Dolly. Teley said you wanted to speak to me."

"Yes, thank you. I'm Tom Casey, private investigator. Would you mind stepping outside."

"Not at all."

In the parking lot, Hawkman showed her the picture. "Do you remember seeing this woman here last Friday night?"

She glanced at the image and nodded. "Oh, yes. That's Destiny. She won a lot of money that night. Well over a thousand dollars."

He furrowed his brow. "You know her personally?"

"No. That's the first time I'd ever seen her."

"But you called her by name."

She laughed. "I have this thing about trying to remember the names of everyone I meet. I use an association method. Most of the time it works, though not always. But it did that night, because I thought of what sort of destination she might take after winning all that money." Then she frowned. "But Teley says she's disappeared."

"Yes. Do you recall if she arrived with anyone?"

"She sat next to Rene. Whether they came together, I really don't know."

"Rene comes often?" Hawkman asked.

She nodded. "Yes, she's a regular."

"Did you notice anyone watching Destiny after she won that money."

"Oh, gosh," she said, scratching the back of her neck. "I wish I could answer that, but I get so busy when the games start I don't notice those types of things." She hesitated a moment then grimaced as she glanced up. "Are you insinuating there's the possibility of foul play?"

"I don't know at this point. We haven't located her car or a body. So the police will probably be out next, as no one has heard from her in three days. The investigation has just started and we're hitting all the angles. Tell me, did you notice any new faces that night other than Destiny's?"

She frowned in thought. tapping a finger on her chin. "You know, now that you mention it, there were a few here Friday that I'd never seen before. But that really isn't unusual. Could just be people visiting relatives or newcomers."

"Did you notice if anyone followed Destiny outside when she left?"

"I call the last set of games and when we end the session, I'm usually so preoccupied with shutting down the computer, that I don't pay attention to people going out the door. But, you might ask Ed or Fred. They're out on the floor cleaning up when everyone leaves."

"Are they here tonight?"

"Yes, I'll relieve Fred" She looked through the glass door and pointed. "And there's Ed. I'll have them come out here where it's quieter."

"Thanks. I'd appreciate that."

Dolly hurried inside. Within a few minutes, two men, one tall, wearing a baseball cap, and the bald headed man that had been dealing out machines, strolled out the door and headed toward him. Hawkman introduced himself.

"I'm Ed," said the tall man. "And this is Fred."

They shook hands. Then Hawkman showed them Destiny's picture. Both remembered seeing her there on Friday night.

"Did either of you notice if she left alone or if someone followed her out?"

"I knew she'd won quite a bit of money and offered to walk her to her car," Ed said. "But she assured me that wouldn't be necessary as she'd parked right in front under the lights and had a friend with her."

"So, you never went outside?"

"Not out the front. I took garbage out the side door to the dumpster," Ed said, pointing toward the corner of the building.

"What about you, Fred?"

"I spotted a jacket she'd left on the chair and dashed out with it just as she started her car."

"Was she alone?" Hawkman asked.

Fred nodded. "Yes."

"Do you remember the make of the vehicle?"

He rubbed his bald head. "A dark green Ford Escort. I remember because it reminded me of one I used to own."

"Did you notice if anyone followed her out of the lot?"

"Cars were lined up to get to the street. I couldn't tell you who pulled out behind her." He looked at Hawkman with a puzzled expression. "Why all the questions about this woman?"

Hawkman stared into his face. "She hasn't been seen since she left this hall."

Eyes wide, Fred stepped back and slapped a fist against his chest. "Oh my God."

CHAPTER FIVE

Hawkman left the bingo hall toying with the possibility that Destiny's car might have been abandoned. He circled several blocks but found no sign of the Ford Escort. He decided to call Rene Taylor at home and ask another question.

"Hello, Rene, Hawkman here."

"I hope you have some good news about Destiny," she said, her voice shaky. "I'm really concerned. Especially since she won the last game of blackout on B-13. And I tell you, the word is spreading like a wildfire that she's missing."

"I don't doubt it," Hawkman said. "Unfortunately, no one I've talked to has seen her since she left the bingo hall. Tell me, did Destiny mention which casino she planned on hitting that night?"

"Yes. The Triple "C", off Interstate 5, just a few miles north of Grants Pass."

"Thanks. I know where it is."

He returned the phone to his belt clip and headed for Interstate 5. With freeway all the way, he made the thirty mile run in twenty minutes. When he pulled into the parking lot of the 'Cow Creek Casino', pegged as the 'Triple "C"' by the locals, he noted in amazement at the number of cars so early on a weekday evening. Inside, he moved past the bodies standing in the aisle playing the slot machines, then wove around the game tables as he hunted for someone who looked like management. He finally spotted an armed security guard who he figured could guide him to an authority figure. The man had his back to him, looking out the glass door toward the outside. Hawkman had to push his way through the crowd and had gotten no more than twenty feet from the uniformed person when someone yelled for help. The guard whirled around and hurried toward the patron.

When Hawkman saw the man's face, his gut tightened. He did a quick turn on his heel, pulled his hat down, and hurried toward the nearest exit. "Damn close call," he muttered.

Back in his truck he breathed a sigh of relief. He'd worked with Max Pritchard at the Agency years ago. What the hell was he doing as a security guard at an Indian casino? Hawkman couldn't expose himself to the man, because as far as most of the Agency knew, he'd been dead for years. Of course, Max wouldn't recognize the name Hawkman nor Tom Casey, the identity he'd been given by the Agency. But he knew his looks hadn't changed that much. He would have known him immediately, as they'd worked together on several cases. It made Hawkman a bit nervous to know someone from his past lived so close. That pretty well settled it. Detective Williams would have to do the questioning at the casino.

Before leaving the parking lot, Hawkman drove through every row searching for Destiny's car. He didn't find anything that even resembled her green Ford Escort. He finally gave up and left.

Tomorrow, he'd call Tom Broadwell, his old boss, and see if he could find out what Pritchard was doing in this neck of the woods. Maybe the guy had retired and needed to supplement his income. But that didn't make sense, as the Agency paid their special agents well. However, one never knew what happened in a person's private life.

While driving home, he called Detective Williams, who knew his history and had been sworn to secrecy. After he explained the situation, Williams assured him that he would stop at the casino that evening and show the enlarged copy of Destiny's picture that Hawkman had given to the police. He'd call later with the results.

That evening, Hawkman and Jennifer strolled out on the deck under a beautiful star lit sky to have their after dinner drink.

He put his arm around her shoulders. "Hey, good-looking, how about a date tomorrow night?"

She stepped back and studied his face. "I see that gleam in your eye. Just what do you have in mind?"

He grinned. "A roaring and exciting night at bingo."

Throwing back her head, she laughed. "Oh, my gosh. I can just see you dabbing numbers." Then her expression turned somber. "This has something to do with Destiny's disappearance, doesn't it?"

He nodded. "Yeah, I want you to help me sort out the people. I met a few of the workers this afternoon. They're quite a comical bunch."

Jennifer smiled. "They're a fun group. I'm not sure I can help you though, since I don't go that often."

"Do you know Argy, Teley, Dolly, Fred, and Ed?"

"Yes, but they're all workers."

"Tell me, how the hell does that woman keep the dark roots of her platinum blond hair from showing? I could look right down at the top of her head and there wasn't a sign of one dark hair."

"It's natural."

Hawkman shot a look at her. "I don't believe it. No woman her age has hair that color without bleaching it."

"It's true. She used to be a red head and has pictures to prove it. When her hair started turning, that's what grew out instead of a mousy gray."

"I'll be damned. I bet she's the envy of many women."

Jennifer laughed. "She is. Me included. But she's a real sweetheart. Bought every one of my books and is waiting for the next one. She also keeps telling me I should write a bingo hall mystery. Maybe it's time to do just that."

Hawkman slapped his forehead. "Oh, no, what ideas have I put into your head?"

She reached up and patted him on the shoulder. "Don't panic, dear. I'll let you know when I start it." Her expression turned somber. "By the way, did you check out the Indian casinos?"

He turned away. "Uh, yeah. But I'm going to let Williams handle that part of the investigation."

Looking puzzled, she walked around and faced him. "Why?"

Shrugging, he took a sip of his drink. "I can't do it all."

She put a hand on her hip. "I've never heard you admit such a thing. So, why all of a sudden is it too much work?"

"Not really. Just figured Williams would do a better job at getting to the casino people."

She frowned. "Hawkman, that's a big fat fib. You might as well clear this up right now, because I won't leave you alone until I hear the reason behind that statement."

He sighed. "You're right. I shouldn't even try that with you. It never works."

After a few moments of silence while he stared across the lake, she tapped her foot and finally poked his arm. "I'm waiting."

Taking a deep breath, he continued. "I went over to the Triple 'C' this afternoon in hopes of finding someone that might have seen Destiny. Instead, I came across a guy that I'd worked with years ago in the Agency. Fortunately, I spotted him before he saw me. I high tailed it out of there as fast as possible."

The thought of someone in Hawkman's past suddenly showing up sent chills down Jennifer's spine. Dirk, the enemy from years ago, who'd stalked Hawkman with the aim to kill, flashed through her mind and her stomach tightened into a knot. She knew as far as most of the Agency was concerned, Hawkman no longer existed, but if some adversary dug deep enough, he might discover that Jim Anderson still lived.

She threaded her arm through his. "Maybe he's just visiting."

He shook his head. "No, he's employed as a gun carrying security guard."

Jennifer cringed. "How dangerous do you think it is to have someone who knew you so close?"

He patted her hand. "Not sure there's any danger. Just makes me nervous."

"When you worked together, did you get along?"

"We had no problems and Max is an excellent agent. It just baffles me that he's working as a guard at a casino. Unless, of course, he's on a case."

"Can you find out?"

"Maybe Broadwell can shed some light on the matter. I'll call him tomorrow."

About that time, he heard the phone ringing and hurried inside.

"Hello."

"Hey, Hawkman, Williams here. I may have our first lead. At least a start."

Grabbing a pencil and paper, he sat down at the kitchen bar. "Shoot."

"One of the cashiers at the casino thinks, but isn't positive, that Destiny cashed in a thousand dollar jackpot."

Hawkman let out a long whistle. "What's the cut-off amount before they have to fill out the 1099 form?"

"Twelve hundred. I had them check their records for that night, but nothing with her name showed up."

'That's too bad. At least we'd know for sure that she made it that far. Still means that if she didn't use up all her bingo winnings that she had about two thousand dollars or more in her possession. Lot of cash for a young woman by herself."

"In a casino at that. Hard to say if anyone noticed or if she had it hidden from sight. I did manage to get some names of people who are considered regulars."

"Roll them by me."

The detective rattled off several unfamiliar names, but the last two impacted Hawkman. "Did you say, Roland Alexander and Rene Taylor?"

"Yes. But these are just a few of those who frequent the casino more often than others. No one could say for sure whether they were there that Friday night."

"That's interesting. Might have to get more specifics on those two."

CHAPTER SIX

The next morning, Hawkman called Tom Broadwell, his old boss at the Agency. They'd kept in close contact throughout the years. Tom badgered him constantly to return to his old job, but the thought of sitting at a desk instead of being in the field didn't appeal to Hawkman.

He could hear the phone call being rerouted through a series of beeps and squawks. When Tom finally answered, he sounded as if he were in a barrel.

"Where the hell are you?" Hawkman asked.

"Don't ask. Good hearing from you. What's up?"

"I need some information on Max Pritchard, but it doesn't sound like you're near a computer."

"You got that right," he laughed. "I haven't seen Max for some time. He might have retired. Why the interest?"

"Spotted him in my area. Curious as to why he's in this neck of the woods. I don't want to blow my cover after all these years."

"Understood. I'll see what I can find out and get back to you as soon as I can."

"Thanks, Tom." Hawkman hung up, a bit frustrated that he'd have to wait for the information.

Jennifer glanced up from her computer. Doesn't sound like you found out much."

He sighed. "Nope. He must be out in the field. Said he'd get back to me later." Hawkman stood and faced her. "By the way, what time should we show up at the bingo hall tonight?"

"Oh, somewhere between five and five thirty. They start

at six thirty and an hour will provide plenty of time for me to teach you the ropes."

"Could you meet me there? Each day that goes by without any word from or about Destiny makes the chances slimmer of our finding her alive. I need to do some heavy footwork fast."

"Sure, I'll see you at the hall about five fifteen."

Hawkman left the house and headed for Medford. He stopped by Barney & Baker Law Offices, only to find that Rene had called in sick and wouldn't be in until the next day. He looked up her address in the phone book and drove over to her place.

When he parked at the curb, he spotted Rene digging in one of her front yard flower beds. As he approached, he could hear her humming and figured she hadn't heard him coming, so he cleared his throat. "Ump. Hello, Rene."

She jumped and dropped the garden trowel. Her dirt-covered hand went to her throat, leaving a smudge on her neck. "Good Lord, you scared me half to death."

"Sorry, didn't mean to startle you."

Rising to her feet, she wiped her hands on an old rag hanging from her waist. "So what brings you out here?"

"I stopped by the law office and they said you were ill. You look pretty good to me."

"Oh, I'm fine, but my little girl is not feeling well. I decided I'd better stay home with her."

"I wanted to ask you some more questions about Destiny."

She clicked her tongue and brushed the back of her hand across her forehead. "Still nothing?"

Hawkman shook his head. "I understand you go out to the Triple 'C' quite often."

She grinned. "Yeah, it's a lot of fun."

"Did Destiny ever go with you?"

She sighed. "Like I told you, that girl never went anywhere. She just went to work and home. Took care of her daddy and that little girl."

"Did she ever speak of being frightened?"

"You mean of a person?"

"Yes."

"She didn't like some people, but as far as I know, she never appeared scared of anyone."

"Who didn't she like?"

"The Alexanders for one. But nobody likes them. They think just 'cause they have a little money that they're better than the rest of us. And she hated the son, Roland."

Hawkman furrowed his brow. "I won't keep you any longer, Rene. Thanks for your time."

She reached out and took hold of Hawkman's arm. "That statement about the Alexanders bothered you didn't it?"

"Not really. I've heard it from others."

"Will you keep me posted on Destiny? I'm really worried. I'm afraid something terrible has happened."

He patted her hand. "Yes, I'll keep you informed."

When he pulled away from the house, her words kept ringing in his ears: 'something terrible has happened'. He didn't want to believe it, but each hour with no word, made it ring truer.

As he drove toward the Alexander's ranch, he thought about Rene's comments regarding that family. He remembered a few years back when he'd heard about the elder Alexander making a killing in the stock market. He'd bought and sold at the right time. They were now living off those profits along with the proceeds he made from raising and selling cattle. The Alexanders had definitely done well.

He reached the white fence that surrounded their place and turned into the long driveway leading to the ranch style home. The grounds were well manicured and pleasing to the eye. Pulling to a stop in front of the house, he heard the barking and baying of dogs. Since none ran out, he assumed they were kept somewhere in a kennel at the rear of the property.

The driveway curved around the main house and continued toward a sizable building that sat back and to the side. The architecture matched that of the house, so he assumed it to be the garage as several domestic and farm vehicles were parked around it.

Hawkman hopped out of his 4X4 and headed toward the large porch that extended across the full length of the house, decorated with a criss-cross wooden border. Lounges, wicker chairs, and small tables lined the area. He walked up the entrance steps which were flanked with square planter boxes filled with colorful flowers. When he punched the bell, he could hear the chimes echoing throughout the house.

Within a few moments, the sound of high heels clicking across a tile floor met his ears. A profoundly beautiful woman in her early twenties opened the door.

"Yes, can I help you?"

"Hello, I'm Tom Casey, a private investigator, looking into the disappearance of Destiny Wilson. I'd like to speak with Roland if he's available."

About that time, a booming voice reverberated from the back of the house. "Who's at the door, Charmaine?" A large man rounded the corner of the living room and headed toward the entry.

"Here comes my daddy. He can answer your questions."

The girl backed away as the man approached. His attire consisted of a red plaid western type shirt, jeans and cowboy boots. Pulling off a pair of leather gloves, he stuck them in his back pocket. "And may I ask who we have here?"

"His name is Tom Casey," she said, turning to leave. "Says he's a private investigator looking into the disappearance of Destiny Wilson. He wants to talk to Roland."

"I've heard of you. Come in," he motioned.

"Thank you, Mr. Alexander," Hawkman said, stepping inside.

"Call me Wallace." He led the way into a huge living room with a vaulted ceiling. "Now, what's this about wanting to see my son?" he asked, sitting down on a large leather couch. "He certainly didn't have anything to do with Destiny's disappearance."

Hawkman took the matching chair, a large marble coffee table separating the two. "I'd like to ask him about the last time he saw her."

"Why, I don't think he's seen that girl in two years."

"From what I understand," Hawkman said, scooting to the edge of the seat, "he's called on Destiny at her home a couple of times within the last month. Also made phone calls to her."

Wallace raised his brows. "I see. And where did you get that information."

"Jesse Wilson. That's why I'd like to speak to Roland."

"The boy's out of town today, taking care of some business. I'll have him get in touch with you as soon as he returns." Wallace stood up, signaling that the conversation had ended.

Hawkman fished out a business card from his pocket and handed it to him. "Have Roland call me, and we'll set up an appointment."

Wallace took the card and tossed it on the coffee table. "I'll do that."

Driving away from the house, Hawkman glanced into his rear view mirror and could see Mr. Alexander standing on the porch watching him drive from the premises. Odd behavior, he thought, that is if there's nothing to hide.

He turned toward the Wilson farm and drove up close to the house. The old hound dog still lay on the porch and howled mournfully when Hawkman came to a stop.

Jesse met him at the door, a glow of expectation in his eyes. "You got good news, I hope."

"Sorry, Jesse. I thought you might have heard something."

The old man lowered his eyes. "Nothing."

Amanda ran into the room, dragging her rag doll. "Hi, Mr. Hawk Man."

"Hello there, pretty little girl. And how are you?"

"I'm fine, but I miss my mommy. She's been gone a long time."

Hawkman gave her a hug. "I'm sure she'll be back soon."

Amanda grabbed a coloring book from the couch and scooted off toward her room. Jesse watched her with sad eyes.

"I spoke with Mr. Alexander a little while ago," Hawkman said. "I really wanted to talk with Roland, but he's out of town."

A flicker of fear passed over Jesse's face.

"Don't worry, you can trust me. At this time I'm not going to bring up Amanda in the conversation. I just want to find out the last time the young man had any contact with Destiny."

"I know you'll do what's best," Jesse said. "I just don't like it."

He patted the old man's shoulder. "I'll keep in touch."

"Amanda," Jesse called, "come say goodbye to Mr. Hawkman."

When he left the house and climbed into his 4X4, Rochester let out a mournful howl that sent chills up his spine. As he drove down the road, he glanced in his side mirror and could see Jesse and Amanda still waving at him from the porch. It made his heart squeeze.

Checking his watch, he figured he had enough time to drop by his office before meeting Jennifer at the bingo hall. He parked and took the stairs two at a time. A gust of hot air hit him when he stepped inside. Immediately, he opened the windows before sitting down.

Once at the desk, he noticed there were five messages on his answering machine, an unusual number for one day. He punched the button and discovered three hang-ups, a client who wanted to know the balance of their bill, then . . . "Hey, private investigator. This is Roland Alexander. I'm a bit pissed that you went to my daddy's house and told him I'd seen Destiny. You and old Jesse better keep your mouth shut from here on out. It ain't none of my daddy's business who I see. If you want to talk to me, call me on my cell phone." He gave the number and the line went dead.

Hawkman leaned back in his chair and stared at the phone number he'd jotted down. Did he want to return the call or let the young Alexander stew awhile. Even though he'd never met him, the tone of voice and the message gave him a good sense of why Destiny wanted nothing to do with this very self absorbed man. But the question still lurked in the back of Hawkman's mind. Did Roland know that Amanda was his child?

CHAPTER SEVEN

Before Hawkman had a chance to give this thought any consideration, his office door burst open and a young black man entered the room, his brown eyes blazing with anger.

However, he stopped dead in his tracks when he spotted the .45 magnum pointing straight at his chest.

"You don't burst into a private investigator's office like a mad bull unless you want to get shot," Hawkman stated, never taking his gaze off the man's face. "Who are you and what do you want?"

"I'm Roland Alexander."

"So, you're the one who left that angry message on my machine? Thought you were out of town for the day."

"Yeah, whatever. You had no business talking to my Pa. You should have come to me."

Hawkman holstered his gun. "I went to the ranch to find you. Your dad asked me why I wanted to see you and I told him. So, why are you so reluctant to let your own father know that you'd seen Destiny?"

"He doesn't think she's worthy of me."

"I see. And how do you feel?"

"That's none of your business."

"It may not be mine, but it's in hands of the authorities now. And the police will make it their business whether you like it or not."

"I don't know nothin' about Destiny's disappearance."

"When did you see her last?"

"I don't have to answer any of your questions."

"That's true. But I've been hired to find her. If you don't

want to cooperate, then it will more than likely put you under heavy suspicion."

The fire in Roland's eyes slowly turned to fear and he moved closer to the desk. "Look, I've tried to see Destiny several times, but she won't have a thing to do with me."

"From what I understand, you're very persistent. Why?"

He shrugged. "Hey, she's a good lookin' babe."

"I thought you were married?"

Roland squared his shoulders. "I ain't anymore, okay. And I found out Destiny ain't as easy as she used to be in high school. Since she had that kid, she's changed."

"I thought the child belonged to a cousin and Destiny's raising her."

"I'm not sure about that. I think the brat's hers."

Glaring at the young man, Hawkman stood. "I have an appointment. If you want to talk about this some more, stop by tomorrow morning. I'll be here."

Roland left the office more subdued. Hawkman crossed to the window and watched him drive away in a sporty red Porsche convertible. He doubted Roland had bought that toy. It more than likely came from his dad. Hawkman sighed in disgust, locked up the office and headed for the bingo hall.

When he entered the White Oak building at five thirty, he spotted Jennifer at one of the aisle tables in the smoking section sitting with her friends. As he approached, he noticed her books displayed on the end and paused for a moment, then pointed at the exhibit. "They allow you to do this?"

"Oh, sure. But, I asked permission first."

"Has it helped your sales?"

"Some of my best customers are bingo players."

He shrugged and sat down beside her where she had provided him with two bingo machines and a set of papers.

"How come you're late?"

"Had an interesting visitor show up at my office."

Her hazel eyes twinkled. "Who?"

"I'll explain later."

"Want a bite to eat before I tell you how these gadgets work?"

"No, thanks. I'm fine for now."

After Jennifer gave him instructions on how to operate the computer devices and coached him on the papers, Hawkman had time to survey the crowd before the games kicked off.

The aroma of popcorn circling his nose prompted him to check its origin. He soon spotted the machine at the far side of the room. A burly looking guy about five foot eight or nine, with a bald head, except for a long braid that looked like it grew from a hole in the back of his head, appeared to be manning the operation. He wore a muscle shirt and his huge arms were littered with tattoos, reminding Hawkman of a Harley motorcycle rider. He turned to Jennifer and whispered. "Who's that guy taking care of the popcorn sales?"

"That's Bruno. He's a volunteer. The popcorn's free. Want me to get us a couple of sacks?"

"I don't think I'd want to meet him in an alley unless I had my gun."

Jennifer laughed. "He's a mean looking bear with a soft heart. You couldn't find a nicer, more polite guy. He opens the door for all the women and carries the bingo machines to the tables for the older people or the handicapped. He's just a sweetheart. Everyone loves him." She pointed to the table in front of the popcorn apparatus. "That's his wife, Penny and she's just as nice. They're a great pair."

Hawkman eyed him suspiciously. "I'll get the popcorn."

When he approached, Bruno stood in front of the machine and raised a hand. "Just a moment, sir. Let it finish popping. I don't want you to get burned."

"Sure," Hawkman said, as he picked up a couple of small paper bags lying on the top of the contraption. "Do you oversee this every night?"

Bruno nodded. "Yeah, this is a good group. I enjoy it."

"Were you here last Friday night?"

"Yep."

Hawkman pulled the picture of Destiny from his pocket and handed it to him. "Do you remember this young woman?"

The broad shouldered man studied the photo for several seconds. "Nope, I don't recall seeing her." He raised a hand. "But let me ask my wife."

He turned toward the tiny woman sitting at the table and showed her the picture. She glanced up at Hawkman and shook her head. "I don't remember her. But we have to stay pretty close to the popcorn and don't stray too far unless we go outside for the break. So it doesn't mean she wasn't here. We just might not have seen her."

Bruno gave back the photo and shrugged. "Sorry we couldn't help."

"Thanks." Hawkman slipped it back into his pocket, then filled the two bags with popcorn and journeyed back to his seat. While munching on the snack, he gazed about the room. He noticed a tall young man with greasy blond, shoulder length hair enter the hall. The newcomer wore a frayed baseball cap backwards, with twigs of hair sticking out the opening on his forehead. His vinyl vest had spots spattered down the front and his jeans were so filthy they looked like they could have stood in the corner by themselves.

Hawkman nudged Jennifer. "Who's that guy?"

She glanced up and frowned. "I don't know if it's his real name, but everyone calls him Tony. He plays bingo all over the area, even in the afternoons. No one is sure if he works."

"Does he play the machines?"

"Oh, yeah."

"How does he afford it?"

She shrugged. "Maybe he inherited his money or is independently wealthy from a dot com operation."

He noticed the unusual blue eyes of the man as he glanced around the room. When his gaze met Hawkman's, he jerked his body backward and rushed toward the far corner of the hall. Hawkman made a mental note to speak to this person tonight.

Watching Argy selling flash boards distracted his mind from the game. The man's antics kept him smiling. When a person called for flashes, Argy would shout, "Raise your hand, not your finger" or "stand up. I'm short." But the comment that made Hawkman chuckle the loudest occurred when a woman almost stepped on the funny man's heels. He turned and looked her in the eye. "Don't follow me, I'm lost."

He leaned toward Jennifer. "How do you concentrate on what's going on? This is like a three ring circus."

The words had barely left Hawkman's mouth, when a tall good looking guy entered from outside. "I'm back!" he called. "I hear voices."

Jennifer glanced up and smiled. "That's Elvis. He's such a doll."

He headed straight for their table. "Don't move, I'm coming." When he reached them, he immediately leaned toward Jennifer. "Hello, beautiful. I still love you."

Hawkman immediately shot him a look. "Uh, oh," Elvis said, backing away, fingering his new growth of beard and mustache. "Is this big ugly guy yours?"

Jennifer laughed. "Yep. Elvis, meet Hawkman."

Elvis put his hands up in mock defense. "Don't worry, I talk to all the beautiful women like that. He held a stack of flash boards. "You want some of these? They're called 'Seasons'. You can win a thousand dollars. Of course," he said with a wink, "if you don't win, you lose."

After he left and proceeded down the aisle, Hawkman shot Jennifer a hard look. "I don't think he's so cute."

She chuckled and patted his curled fist. "I'm glad, dear. Now lighten up. We're here to have fun."

At the break, Hawkman noticed that Tony, knocking a pack of cigarettes against his hand, went outside. He immediately got up and followed the dirty man. When he reached the patio area, he searched the crowd and finally spotted Tony heading down the drive away from the group. He had the feeling this character didn't want to be approached, but he pursued him anyway. "Hi, my wife tells me you play a lot of bingo. I'm new at this game and don't know what I'm doing. Can a guy win much money here?"

The man glared at him, but nodded. "Yeah, I'm lucky."

"That's good. Maybe I'll have some beginner's luck." He pulled the picture of Destiny from his pocket. "Since you're a regular player, did you see this woman here last Friday night?"

He gave Hawkman a questioning glance. "Who are you?"

"I'm a private investigator. She's disappeared and I've been hired to find her."

The coloring around the man's mouth turned almost green as he glanced at the photo.

"Yeah, I sat right next to her."

"Then you're aware that she won quite a bit of money?"

"So? Everyone else knew it too."

"Did she mention that she planned on going to an Indian casino after bingo?"

"I think she said something like that."

"Did you by any chance see her at the casino?"

His eyes narrowed. "I don't like the tone of that question. In fact, I'm not answering any more." He threw down his cigarette, crushed the butt with his heel and hurried back inside.

Hawkman sauntered in a few seconds later and joined Jennifer. Surveying the room, he couldn't find the long-haired guy. "Did you happen to notice where Tony went?"

Jennifer pointed toward the back door. "He gathered up his stuff and scurried out that way."

He jumped up. "I'll see you at home."

Jennifer grabbed his arm. "But what about the rest of the games?"

He patted her hand. "You'll have to play them without me, love. I may have found a lead." He left the table and hurried toward the exit.

CHAPTER EIGHT

Once outside, Hawkman raced around the corner of the building and spotted the taillights of a Dodge pick-up as it backed out of a parking spot. He ran toward the vehicle waving his arms. The driver gunned the engine and headed straight toward him. Hawkman leaped between two cars to keep from being run down. The truck screeched around the corner and swerved dangerously close to other cars as it headed for the exit.

Hawkman dashed to his 4X4 and jumped inside. But by the time he reached the street, the vehicle had disappeared. He slapped the steering wheel with his hand. "Damn!"

The numbers on the Dodge's license plate were partially blocked by clumps of dirt, but he jotted down what he could see. He drove in several directions, checking side streets and driveways, but saw nothing. Tony had panicked when he'd mentioned Destiny. Why? Did he have something to hide? He needed more information about this man.

Hawkman returned to the bingo hall and made a direct line for the office area. He motioned for the manager to meet him outside. Within a few minutes, Teley joined him on the front patio.

"Is there news about the disappearance of that young woman?" Teley asked.

"Nothing. But I'd like to inquire about one of your regular customers known as Tony."

Teley shrugged. "All we know about him is that he answers to that name. He spends lots of money and, of course, we like that."

"Has he ever written a personal check to the hall?"

He shook his head. "No, we don't accept them anymore. Too many bounced and we were losing money. However, we do have an ATM, but that doesn't give us much information." He rubbed his chin. "Come to think of it, I've never seen him use that either. He seems to always have cash on hand."

"So you don't know his last name?"

"Nope, but, I'll ask around."

"Thanks, I'd appreciate it."

The two men walked back into the hall, and Teley veered off toward the office, as Hawkman headed back to his seat next to Jennifer.

"What was that all about?" she asked.

"My lead escaped. I'll explain later. Have you won?"

She smiled. "Yep. Five hundred dollars on Double Dab."

Hawkman raised his brows. "Wow! Really?"

She patted her pocket. "I wouldn't kid you about that." She scooted his machines and papers in front of him. "Here, play your own stuff now. We only have a few more games left."

He glanced up at the caller's seat to see Dolly, the blond haired woman, with microphone in hand. She adjusted the chair to fit her short body, then smiled at the audience. "This is the time I remind you to place your trash sacks on the table before leaving. It really helps us get out of here earlier and it's much appreciated. Please keep your hands and feet inside the vehicle, enjoy the ride and don't take off your seat belts until we've come to a complete stop." She placed one of the small round balls into the view finder and glanced up as a little old lady, popping her cane against the floor, ran rapidly across the room to her seat. "Ida, no running in the hall."

The players burst into laugher.

Hawkman shot a look at Jennifer and raised a brow.

She waved a hand in the air and laughed. "Don't worry about it. It's just all in fun." Then she pointed to his machine. "Punch in B-13, that's the first number of this game, then mark it on your papers."

Jennifer rolled her eyes at her friends as Hawkman fumbled

with the dauber cap and finally got the number marked. Smothered giggles were heard around the table.

After the last game called Blackout, Hawkman carried Jennifer's bundle of books to her van, then followed her home. Once they arrived and had everything put away, Hawkman headed for his computer in the spare bedroom that he'd turned into an office. Before he could get settled, Jennifer poked her head around the door. "Oh, you forgot to tell me about the interesting visitor you had this afternoon. Also, why did you dash out of the hall after Tony?"

He related the story about Roland, and she looked at him in surprise. "Hasn't it occurred to you that he suspects Amanda is his child? That's why he doesn't want anything about Destiny brought to his dad's attention."

Hawkman scratched his sideburn. "Yes. The thought did pass through my mind, but let's keep it to ourselves." It amazed him how Jennifer's intuition always found its mark.

"Don't worry about me. I'm not one to spread rumors. You know how I hate gossip." She turned away, then whirled back around. "Oh, and why did you go chasing Tony?"

"He acted mighty suspicious when I questioned him about Destiny at the break. So when you said he'd left, I wanted to check out why. But, after trying to run me down, he disappeared."

Jennifer put her hand to her mouth. "You're kidding? He actually tried to hit you with his vehicle?"

"Yep."

"Even though he looks scraggy, I never thought of him as the violent type."

"When you're pushed into a corner, there are a lot of actions you might take that you normally wouldn't. When I showed him Destiny's picture and said she'd disappeared, the guy came unglued. I think he knows something."

"I saw you talking to Teley. Were you asking about Tony?"

He nodded. "But none of the workers know anything more than he answers to that name and spends lots of money." He waved a piece of paper at her. "However, I did manage to get a partial license plate number. I'm going to see if Stan can help me out."

Jennifer headed for the bedroom, mumbling. "Goes to show you never know what goes on in people's heads."

Hawkman booted up the computer and sent an e-mail to Stan, a retired cop who volunteered at the police department and had helped him out on numerous cases. Hawkman asked him to run the partial plate number through the system and see what he could come up with. He didn't expect an answer that night, so he shut down and went to bed.

The next morning, Hawkman grabbed a cup of coffee and went straight to the computer. He stared at the screen as it came to life hoping there would be a message. Sure enough, the first post listed came from the police department. Stan had compiled several names along with the types of vehicles that had the partial license numbers he'd sent. The name Tony Ricardo, who owned a Dodge Ram, grabbed Hawkman's interest. He immediately e-mailed Stan, asking if he could do a search on this one and send him the stats A.S.A.P.

He put the computer in sleep mode, ate breakfast and called Detective Williams. Unfortunately, the detective had nothing new to report. They hadn't found Destiny's car, nor did he have any more information from the bingo hall or casino people. They'd pretty much hit a dead end. He'd sent her picture out on the national wire and hoped he'd get some results soon.

Hawkman related the incident with Tony at the bingo hall the night before and Williams showed an interest.

"I asked Stan to run a check on the partial license plate number I'd acquired," Hawkman said. "He sent a list and a guy with the name Tony Ricardo with an identical vehicle piqued my interest. Now he's running another check on that individual. I should be hearing from him soon."

"Let me know when you get that information. Then I'll run the name through our system."

After hanging up with Williams, Hawkman dialed Jesse, then wished he hadn't. The poor man sounded on the brink of tears while talking about Destiny.

"I know that as each day goes by, the percentages go down on finding my girl alive," he groaned.

"Now, Jesse, that isn't always the case," Hawkman said in a strong voice, but figured his efforts fell on deaf ears. "I've got a few leads that I'm going to follow up today. I don't want you to despair, you hear? You have to stay strong for Amanda."

"I know, I know, but it gets harder as each day passes with no word."

"I promise I'll keep in touch."

Hawkman had no sooner dropped the receiver on the cradle than the phone rang. "Hello."

"Hawkman, Tom Broadwell. I've got some information you might find of interest."

"Shoot."

"I did a run down on Max Pritchard. Turns out he's on an undercover mission. His niece, a brother's daughter, is missing. She liked to gamble and was last seen at the Indian casino in Medford, Oregon. That's why Max is working there as a security guard. He's only been employed a few weeks."

"How old was she?" Hawkman asked.

"Twenty-four."

"That's very interesting."

"Why?"

"I'm also working on a case of a missing twenty-four year old woman who was last seen at a bingo hall."

"Hmm. Maybe you two ought to compare notes."

"Might not be a bad idea. Thanks, Tom, for getting back to me so quickly. Appreciate it."

After hanging up, Hawkman sat in deep thought, drumming his fingers on the counter top. After a few minutes, he hurried back to the computer. Stan hadn't let him down.

CHAPTER NINE

Stan had attached a whole file for Hawkman to examine. The mug shot on the driver's license definitely verified Tony Ricardo as the man at the bingo hall who had tried to run him down in the parking lot.

He printed out the photo and other information contained on the rap sheet. Ricardo had several unpaid moving violations and outstanding parking tickets. Hawkman thought it interesting that an aggravated assault charge had been filed by a woman, but it never went to trial. He wondered why. After going through everything, he jotted down the latest known address and shoved the photo into his pocket.

Since he'd told Roland Alexander that he'd be in his office this morning, he'd better get going in case the man decided to show up. Flopping on his faithful leather cowboy hat, he shrugged into his jeans jacket and headed for Medford.

When he arrived and strolled in front of the donut shop below his office, a wonderful aroma surrounded his nostrils and he couldn't pass by without salivating. Even though Jennifer had warned him of the extra inches he'd gained around his middle, temptation won over her caution. He went inside and bought two cream filled delights, then headed upstairs where he immediately put on the coffee pot. While waiting for the brew, he checked his mail and phone messages. He'd just sunk his teeth into the fluffy pastry when a knock sounded on the door.

Letting out a sigh, he called. "Who's there?"

Roland Alexander poked his head around the edge. "May I come in, Mr. Casey?"

Hawkman immediately noticed the change in attitude from yesterday. He motioned toward the chair in front of his desk. "Have a seat, Mr. Alexander."

The young man crossed the room and sat down. "Call me Roland. Save the Mr. Alexander for my old man."

"Okay, Roland. What can I do for you?"

"I want to clear up some stuff so that you don't think I had something to do with Destiny's disappearance."

"I'm listening."

The young man took a deep breath, then cleared his throat. "Based on the rumors I've heard and what my old man said, Destiny was last seen at the White Oak Bingo Hall on Friday night."

"That's true."

"Well, I saw her after that."

Hawkman leaned forward. "Where?"

"At the Triple 'C'."

"Did you speak with her?"

"No, because I had my sister with me. I'd promised Charmaine that I'd take her to the casino on her birthday. She turned twenty-one on Friday."

"How long did you stay?"

Roland wrinkled his nose and scratched his head. "Oh, I'd say we left about 1:30 AM."

"Did Destiny stay there that long?"

"I don't know. I only saw her once standing in front of the cashier's booth."

"Anyone with her?"

"She stood alone in the line. That's all I know."

Hawkman pulled the picture of Tony Ricardo from his pocket. "Did you by any chance see this man that night?"

Roland frowned then pointed at the picture. "Oh yeah, that guy's always there. He hangs out at every casino and bingo hall in town."

"That's interesting," Hawkman said, sliding the picture back into his pocket. "Did he talk to Destiny?"

He shrugged. "I don't know. He was at one of the poker tables when I saw him."

"Did you speak to him."

Roland shook his head. "No."

"After you took your sister home, where'd you go?"

"Back to my apartment."

"Can you prove it?"

He jerked up his head and looked at him, wide eyed. "No. But, honest, I went straight home and to bed."

"I believe you, but the police will want a better answer. So try to remember anyone who might have seen you or even called you that night so they can verify your whereabouts."

Roland wiped a hand over his face and stared at Hawkman. "Dear God, I swear I had nothin' to do with her disappearance."

"Then pray hard we find her soon."

Hawkman noticed that Roland left his office in a daze. He appeared to be scared. But that could be an act. He still questioned whether the young man had anything to do with Destiny's vanishing. It sure seemed like he wanted to cover his butt.

Once Roland shut the door, Hawkman leaned back in his chair and finished his donuts. After draining the last drop of coffee from his cup, he slid open the desk side drawer and removed his lock-pick case. He stood and slipped on his jacket that he'd draped over the back of the chair, then shoved the kit into the pocket. As he left the office, his thoughts went to what he might find at Tony Ricardo's apartment.

When he reached the complex, he drove through, checking for the Dodge truck. When he didn't see it, he went back out and parked on the street. As he strolled toward the building, he wondered how a guy like Ricardo, with no known employment, could afford the gas for that vehicle he drove. Shaking his head, it amazed him how many luxuries such as big cars, cell phones, huge televisions, booze and cigarettes that people bought, yet cried poor-mouth.

Since the address read 22B, he climbed the outside stairs,

assuming it would be on the second floor. The place appeared in pretty good shape. The locale didn't indicate slum, but couldn't be called upper class either. Hawkman studied the architecture and noted that ten small apartments were housed in this one structure. They definitely couldn't have big interiors, but how much room would a single guy need?

The entries were located down a long hallway in the center of the building. Each door had bold black numbers painted in the middle, making it easy for Hawkman to find the apartment. He knocked and surveyed the area while waiting for an answer. No sounds of talking, television or music came from any of the flats and he didn't see another human on the premises. In fact, the quietness gave him an eerie feeling. He turned toward the door and again knocked softly. When he didn't receive a response this time, he quickly took out his lock pick and in a matter of seconds entered the room.

He quietly clicked the door shut and waited a moment until his vision adjusted to the dimness inside. All the drapes were drawn tight and the thought flashed through his mind that even though he hadn't spotted the Dodge in the parking lot, the guy might be asleep. He could see the small kitchen from where he stood, so the remaining door had to be the bedroom. Advancing cautiously, he peered inside.

A quilt and sheet lay in a rumpled mess on top of the mattress, but nobody occupied the bed. On the far wall of the room, the door to the bathroom stood wide open. Hawkman crossed over to the window and looked out the corner of the drape to the parking lot directly below. So far no Dodge truck had turned up.

He made a quick search of the bedroom, and found a few porno magazines, but it didn't surprise him that a single guy would have dirty books. However, when he slid open the closet door, he discovered a different scene. Hanging on hooks around the edge were handcuffs, leather belts, ropes, a whip, silver and gold fancy chains along with other lewd looking devices. It appeared the guy enjoyed some kinky sex habits.

Hawkman closed the closet, then checked the parking lot

again. He caught his breath when the dark green Dodge pulled up. He only had a few seconds to get out of sight. Noticing the tiny pantry in the kitchen, he prayed it would be big enough. He'd no more stepped inside the little enclosure, mashing against a broom handle that poked him in the back, when he heard the key turn in the lock. He prayed the guy wouldn't be hungry.

Unable to close the door tightly, he peered through the hinged side crack. The same sleazy looking Tony he'd seen at the bingo hall entered the apartment, flipped on the light and scurried toward the bedroom. Hawkman heard the closet door grinding against grit in the runner as it slid open. The hanging items banged and rattled against the wall as Tony fumbled in the closet. Grumbling and cursing loudly, he finally stumbled into the kitchen with a set of chains draped over his arm and handcuffs dangling from his fingers. With his free hand, he scratched his dirty head, glanced around the small room, then headed straight for the pantry.

CHAPTER TEN

Hawkman prepared for a confrontation as he watched the man approach his hiding place. Suddenly, Tony stopped, swooped up a paper sack lying on one of the kitchen chairs and flipped it open. He dropped the fancy chains and cuffs into the bag, folded the top down, turned off the light and headed out of the apartment. Hawkman heard the lock click and breathed a sigh of relief. Staying hidden for a few more moments, he thought about how the man's steely blue eyes glowed in the dim light. It sent a shiver down his spine. He finally ventured out of the small closet and hurried to the draped window. Pulling the curtain back slightly, he watched Tony jump into his truck and speed out of the lot.

Hawkman decided not to follow, since this might be his only opportunity to thoroughly check out the apartment. He hurried back to the bedroom, searched the drawers of the dresser and small bed table, then crossed over to the bathroom where he went through the medicine cabinet. He found several different types of prescription drugs which he recognized as being for pain or sleeping. They were made out to Elsa or Marco Ricardo, and the dosages were high, consistent with those prescribed for someone very sick, deeply injured or terminally ill. Hawkman also noted the doctor's name as Crowley and decided he'd have a talk with this physician. He might not be able to find out much without Detective Williams, but it would be worth a try before having to call the busy detective. He felt the muscles in his jaw tighten. The whole idea that he had to depend on the local police department to help him get his information always stuck in his craw. This wouldn't happen if he were still in the Agency.

He exhaled loudly and decided he'd better leave before people started coming home from work. He slowly opened the door, checked up and down the corridor, then stepped into the hallway.

On his way out, he noticed one of the doors had 'OFFICE' printed in bold black letters and decided to ask some questions about the tenant in 22B. He pulled a pen and small pad of paper from his pocket before knocking. The woman who opened the door wore a bright red bandanna wrapped around curlers in her hair.

"Yeah, whatdaya want?"

Hawkman plastered on his best smile. "Hi. Are you the manager of these apartments?"

"Yeah."

I'm doing a credit check on one of your tenants, Tony Ricardo." He glanced at his pad of paper. "Do you ever have trouble collecting his rent?"

"Tony Ricardo," she repeated, furrowing her brow. "Oh yeah," raising a finger in the air. "Rents out 22B."

"Yes, he's the one."

She shook her head so hard one of the curlers flipped out from underneath her scarf and fell to the floor. "Nope, don't have no problems with him," she grunted, swooping up the plastic roller from the dirty carpet. "Wish all my tenants were like him."

"Oh, why's that?" Hawkman asked.

"Pays on time and ain't around enough to get the place dirty."

"I don't understand. Doesn't he live here?"

"Yeah, some of the time. But he must have a girlfriend he stays with, 'cause he don't sleep here but maybe once or twice a week, if that."

"Ever seen him with a girl?"

"Nope, never brought her around here, that I ever seen."

Hawkman furrowed his brow. "That's odd." Then he smiled

again. "But, I'm only interested in whether he pays his bills and not in his personal life."

"We don't have no problem there. So you can give him a plus from us."

Hawkman touched the brim of his hat. "Thank you, ma'am, appreciate the information."

"You're welcome." And she slammed the door.

He walked back to his truck, contemplating what the woman had said about Tony seldom being there. Where the hell would a man sleep if not at his own apartment? From the reports Hawkman had received up to this point, he certainly didn't appear to have a girlfriend. However, this man had some sort of sadistic quirk. He might have to tail him a couple of nights and find out where he went. Damn! That meant he'd have to go to bingo and follow him from there, since he couldn't depend on Tony coming back to his apartment.

Hawkman made a U-turn and headed for Max Pritchard's address that he'd received form Broadwell the night before. Fearing Pritchard would be shocked as hell to see him standing in front of him, alive and well, he decided to approach him in private instead of at the casino.

Hawkman figured Max would more than likely work evenings since the report stated the last sighting of his niece had occurred during those hours. He hoped he'd calculated the shifts right and that he'd be home.

This apartment complex appeared much more up-scale than the one he'd just left. The grounds were manicured and a fountain occupied the center of the parking lot. Quite a pleasant scene, Hawkman thought, as he pulled into a visitor's parking space.

He quickly surveyed the numbers in gold along the door frame of each entry and spotted Max's apartment on the ground floor. He took a deep breath and approached. In place of a bell, a small gold plated knocker occupied the center of the door. Hawkman rapped it three times, then turned around with his back facing the entry.

"Yes?" a familiar voice asked.

"Sir, you have to the count of three before I blow off your head." Hawkman had just uttered a secret phrase the two of them had used years ago. He slowly turned and looked into the face of his old buddy.

Max's blue eyes were wide and his ruddy complexion had actually turned ashen gray. "My God, am I looking at a ghost?" he muttered. When he finally got his composure back, his huge arms grabbed Hawkman in a bear hug, tears welling in his eyes. "Is it actually you, Jim?"

"Yep. New name though. I'd like you to meet Tom Casey, Private Investigator, known as Hawkman by his friends and relatives."

Wiping his eyes, Max grabbed his shoulder and shoved him inside. "Get your ass in here and tell me what has happened to you after all this time."

Max popped a couple of beers and the two men talked for over an hour, catching up on many lost years. Hawkman asked him to keep his identity secret due to enemies that wanted him dead.

"No problem. You don't know how good it is to see you're still alive. God, I've missed working with you. Best agent in the business."

"Thanks. You weren't so bad yourself. By the way, how's Sheryl?"

Max's lips quivered. "I lost her to cancer two years ago. It's been mighty lonesome. I try to stay as busy as I can."

"I'm sorry to hear that, old friend."

Taking a deep breath, Max changed the subject and pointed at Hawkman's head. "So, the patch is for real? Even though your name and life have changed."

"Yep, detached retina. When I found those two bastards that were involved in murdering Sylvia, I could have killed them with my bare hands. But one of them hit me in the head with a steel pipe. The adrenalin pumped through me so hard that it didn't even phase me at the moment and I shot them both."

"So, it affected you later?"

Hawkman nodded. "My sight turned fuzzy and I noticed a

real sensitivity to light. Even after several surgeries and a steroid shot into my eye, my vision still remained hazy." He shrugged. "So, I slapped a patch on the sucker and that's the way it's been ever since. Of course, I couldn't work in the field anymore and the Agency wanted to put me at a desk. I would have hated that type of a job. So, I retired. Got me a little place at Copco Lake with a new name, a job where I'm the boss, married a beautiful woman and am happy as a clam," he said, with a twinkle in his eye.

Max chuckled. "I can't imagine anything slowing you down. But, tell me, how in the hell did you find me?"

Hawkman told him about the disappearance of Destiny and how he'd traced her to the casino. "When I spotted you there as a security guard, it shocked me. I called Broadwell and he explained your presence. I thought maybe we should compare notes since we have similar cases."

"That's interesting. Another young woman of about the same age has disappeared without a trace." Max frowned. "Doesn't sound good."

"I agree. It's not like we're talking about Los Angeles or San Francisco." Hawkman leaned forward putting his elbows on his knees. "Tell me about your niece."

CHAPTER ELEVEN

Smoothing back a thick mass of dark brown hair sprinkled with gray, Max Pritchard let out a sigh. "Carmen is my brother's oldest daughter and my favorite of his three girls. Of course, I wouldn't tell the other two that, but Carmen's feisty personality kept everyone in the family on their toes. She also drove her folks crazy with her bull-headed ways. When she reached sixteen and started dating, I thought my brother would lose his cool and kill her. The guys she brought home were the lowest form of life; covered with tattoos, pierced body parts and wearing low-slung pants. Just creeps! Some even had police records." He ran a hand over his chin and grimaced.

"Being a cop, my brother Joe questioned these young hoodlums until Carmen swore she'd never bring another one home. She told her dad they might not look like ivy leaguers, but they were nice to her. Joe couldn't understand it. Carmen was beautiful, and he couldn't imagine why she had so much trouble attracting a decent guy." Max leaned back on the couch and threw up his hands in despair.

"However, he'd heard unpleasant rumors about his daughter and feared she'd established a bad reputation. He reluctantly admitted that these types of young men might be the only ones who would give her a second look."

Hawkman thought about how Carmen's background seemed similar to that of Destiny's. "Now these incidents occurred when she went to high school, right?"

He nodded. "Yes. She attended the public school here in Medford. In fact, Joe still lives here. His second daughter got married and moved back east, but the youngest is still home."

"So what happened to Carmen?"

"The minute she turned eighteen, she left without giving any warning or forwarding address. No one heard from her for several months. Then one day, she called Joe collect. In tears, she begged him to let her come home. Even though it relieved him to hear her voice and know she was alive, he didn't trust her. He told her she could come back, but only on the condition that she'd abide by their rules, which she agreed to do eagerly."

"It would be hard for a parent to turn down that plea."

Max nodded. "Joe told me when he picked her up at the bus depot the next day, he couldn't believe her appearance. She looked ill, her big green eyes didn't sparkle and she'd lost so much weight he hardly recognized her. Her beautiful long blond hair hung in greasy strands down her back. She stunk as if she hadn't had a bath in weeks."

"Where the hell had she been?" Hawkman asked.

"Some commune in Nevada. They wouldn't let her leave, so she had to sneak away in the middle of the night. She caught a ride with some trucker who gladly let her off at a bus depot, even gave her money for the trip home." Max shook his head. "He either felt sorry for her or couldn't stand the smell."

"Sounds like she got involved with a cult."

"Yep. That's exactly what happened. One of those low-life boyfriends told her about this bunch. He fed her a tale of how life would be so much better with this group and convinced her to leave home to go with him. Carmen told her dad, that this group practiced devil worship and experimented with kinky sex. The whole ordeal scared the hell out of her."

"Good Lord, I can see why." Lifting off his cowboy hat, Hawkman ran a hand through his hair, then plopped it back on his head. "So she's lived at home since this happened?"

Max took a deep breath and leaned back on the couch. "She got a job, paid rent to her folks and turned into a decent person. I think that experience really matured her. But then, she disappeared and no one has heard from her in over three weeks. The police haven't shown much interest because of her background. They figure she headed back to the cult."

"What do you think?"

"I think she's been kidnapped."

Hawkman raised a brow. "What makes you think that?"

"I investigated that cult and they don't exist anymore. Nevada police shut them down a year ago and the leaders are in jail. Also, her car hasn't been found."

"You said she was last seen at the casino."

"One of her weaknesses. She loved to play the slots and had damned good luck. The night she disappeared, she'd won five thousand dollars on one machine. And the odd thing was, she took a check for the money and it hasn't been cashed. Makes me throw robbery to the bottom of the pile."

"What do you put at the top?"

"Damned if I know. I'm completely baffled."

Hawkman leaned back and rubbed a hand over the stubble on his chin. "There are a lot of similarities to these two cases. Especially with both girls winning a hunk of money and their cars disappearing without a trace. That seems strange. You'd think the vehicles would show up somewhere, deserted, or sold."

"Yeah, my thinking too." Max glanced at his watch and jumped up. "Damn, I've got to get to work."

Hawkman stood. "I'll get back with you either tonight at the casino or tomorrow morning. Maybe by working together, we can find the girls."

Max put out his hand. "I'm all for it. It'll be like the good old days. Sure good having you back on my team."

Standing, they shook hands, both grinning. "Like old times, buddy," Hawkman said, slapping Max on the back.

The days were growing longer, but by the time Hawkman reached Jesse's place the sun had set. Rochester, in his usual spot, lifted his snout and let out a mournful howl when the investigator approached the steps. Hawkman knelt down and rubbed the dog between the ears. "You still waiting for Destiny, old boy?"

The dog thumped his tail on the wood planks, let out a whine, then dropped his head back onto his paws.

Jesse opened the screen door. "That dog will barely eat. And I can't coach him inside. I don't know what I'm going to do with him."

"He'll come around." Hawkman stood and hooked his thumbs in his front jeans pockets.

"Any news?" Jesse asked.

"Nothin' yet. But I'm making a little headway. Need to ask you a few questions."

"Sure, I'll do anything to help. Come on in," he said, holding the screen open with his cane.

Hawkman sniffed the aroma of a beef roast and home baked bread. "Man, this house always smells good."

Jesse chuckled. "I have a feeling the way to your heart is through your stomach. I've never seen a man enjoy the smell of good food as much as you do."

Hawkman laughed aloud. "You sound like Jennifer. That's the way she gets me up in the morning. Bacon, eggs and toast. Hmm!" he said, rubbing his stomach.

Grinning, Jessie shook his head and started to sit down.

"Wait," Hawkman said, raising a hand. "Before you get comfortable. Did Destiny buy her school's yearbooks?"

"Yeah, I think she's got them all."

"Can you lay your hands on them right now without having to dig in a storage box?"

He nodded. "She always kept them on the shelves by her bed. In fact, she has them all. So which one do you want to see?"

"Bring the last three."

Within a few minutes Jesse limped back into the room with Amanda running ahead of him carrying the three books.

"Hi, Mr. Hawk Man," she said, placing them beside him on the couch.

He smiled and gave her a hug. "How's the prettiest little girl on the block?"

"I'm fine. Would you please excuse me? I'm watching television in my Mommy's room and it's my favorite program."

"Certainly," Hawkman said smiling. He glanced up at Jesse. "She's not only pretty, she has good etiquette."

"Destiny is a stickler for manners. She says they don't hurt nobody." Jesse lowered himself carefully into the straight back chair. "Now why is it you want to see those?"

"I've discovered another young woman has disappeared from this area. She went to the same school as Destiny and is approximately the same age. I'd like to see if there could be a link between the two."

"What's her name?"

"Carmen Pritchard."

Jesse's eyes narrowed. "She's missing too?"

Hawkman's jerked up his head and stared at Jesse. "You know her?"

"Wild as a hare in high school. Don't know much about her now. She might have changed like my Destiny did. The last I heard she'd run away, but had come back home. I haven't seen her in a long time and don't recall Destiny mentioning her lately. The two girls ran around together for a short time in school, but she even scared my daughter."

Hawkman furrowed his brows. "How?"

"Don't rightly know. Just one day, Destiny told me she didn't want to be seen with her anymore because she did scary stuff. She never would tell me what frightened her about the girl. But I figured it must be pretty bad if Destiny didn't want any part of it."

Hawkman had been thumbing through the yearbook as they talked and came across the senior picture of Carmen Pritchard. He held it up and pointed to the photo. "Is this her?"

Jesse nodded. "Yep. A beautiful young woman."

"I can see that." But Hawkman noticed the green eyes of the girl. They looked as if they were casting a spell on the photographer as she stared into the camera.

He flipped through the pages and a loose photo floated

out onto the floor. Hawkman reached down and picked it up. When he started to slip it back between the pages, he stiffened in shock.

CHAPTER TWELVE

Hawkman stared at the senior prom picture: Tony Ricardo, decked out in a formal tuxedo, a big grin on his face and an arm around Destiny's waist. He glanced at Jesse and held the picture toward him. You know this fellow?

Jesse frowned. "Not really. That's the only time I ever saw the young man. He picked up Destiny for the dance, but he never came around anymore. In fact, I don't even remember his name."

"Tony Ricardo."

"Yeah, that's right." He glanced at Hawkman with a puzzled expression. "How'd you know?"

"I questioned him at the bingo hall. He sat next to Destiny last Friday night."

"You're kidding." Jesse held out his hand. "Let me see that picture again."

Hawkman gave it to him and watched as he studied the photo. The old fellow soon shook his head. "Nope, haven't seen him around here since that night." He scratched his chin. "Funny, don't even recall Destiny saying whether she had a good time or not at the prom."

"That's not important. What I find interesting is that they've known each other for several years." Hawkman continued to turn the pages and soon found Tony's senior picture. "Looks like he might have been a pretty clean-cut kid at one time. You should see him now. He's a dirty slob."

Jesse shifted his weight in the chair and grimaced in pain.

Hawkman jumped up and moved to his side. "You okay?"

"Yeah, just got myself in a bit of a bind. I'll be fine in a minute."

Sitting back down on the couch, Hawkman scowled. "Wish you'd go see a doctor, you stubborn old cuss."

Chuckling, Jesse pointed a shaky finger at him. "You mind your own business, you young whipper snapper."

Hawkman slid the photo into the yearbook and held it up. "Can I borrow this and the prom picture for a day or two? I want to make some copies. Then I'll bring them back."

"No problem. You take what you need."

Amanda came bounding into the room. "Grandpa, my program's over. I'm ready for my dessert now."

Hawkman stood. "I won't keep you any longer. You've got a pretty little girl there with a sweet tooth. I think she takes after her grandpa," he said, winking at the child.

Amanda giggled and leaned against Jesse, slipping her arm through his. He patted her hand and smiled.

"Yep, we do like that ice cream." He raised his face to the ceiling, closed his eyes and licked his lips. "Hmm, yeah, especially with chocolate dribbled over the top and a sprinkle of nuts." He put the tip of his cane on the floor and used it to stand. "My goodness, we gotta hurry to the kitchen right now."

Hawkman laughed and headed toward the door. "I'll be seeing you Jesse. Good night, Amanda."

She ran to the door and threw him a kiss. He acted like he caught it and slapped it on his cheek. "Don't you tell Jennifer you kissed me. She'll be jealous."

He climbed into the 4X4 and pulled away, watching the young girl in his rear view mirror as she jumped up and down waving from the porch. Rochester stood beside her, his nose in the air, howling a mournful song.

Driving toward town from the Wilson farm, Hawkman decided to drop by the casino before going home. He'd let Max know what he'd uncovered. His gut told him that Destiny, Carmen and Tony had something in common, but what? They'd all grown up together in the same area. The two women appeared to have been a bit wild when young, yet matured into responsible young adults. But Tony had gone in reverse. So what would bind them together? He needed to find out more about Tony. That might hold the key to unlock this puzzle.

He turned into the casino parking lot. But before getting out of the truck, Hawkman called Detective Williams. He caught him at the office. "Don't you ever go home?"

"Isn't this home? I do have another residence that I visit, but I give this as my permanent address."

Hawkman chuckled. "I can see why. Just wanted to touch base with you. Anything new on the Destiny Wilson case?"

"Nothing. It's like the missing person we've had on the books for about three or four weeks. Destiny is the second young woman who's disappeared without a trace in less than two months. It's a bit weird."

"You mean Carmen Pritchard?"

"Yeah, how'd you find out about her?"

"'Cause I'm a good investigator."

Williams let out a loud guffaw. "Right."

"Kidding aside, how long are you going to be there?"

"Probably a couple more hours."

"I'll be by before heading home. I might have something worth looking into."

"Sounds good. See you then."

Hawkman clipped the phone back on his belt, slipped the prom photo out of the yearbook and put it into his shirt pocket, then went into the casino. He strolled around observing the crowd until he spotted Max talking with a customer. He plunked some coins into a slot machine as he waited and won a small jackpot. Max walked up behind him and slapped him on the back.

"Hey, you gambler, what's up?"

"Gotta minute?"

"Yep, I'm due for a break." He pointed toward one of the side entrances. "Meet me outside that door and I'll join you for a smoke."

Hawkman gathered up his winnings and dropped them into one of the casino plastic buckets. He glanced around for a cashier but all the booths had long lines, so he decided to wait until after he talked to Max before cashing in. He ambled outside and within a few seconds Max joined him, lit a cigarette and held the pack toward Hawkman. But he quickly slipped them back into his pocket. "Sorry, forgot you'd quit."

"Yeah. Still crave them though." Sticking a toothpick into his mouth, he smiled. "Doesn't taste the same but it's better than nothing."

Max grinned. "So, you find out anything?"

Hawkman told him about the two girls being acquainted, then told him about Tony Ricardo escorting Destiny to the senior prom. He showed him the photo and then the recent shot taken off of Tony's driver's license. "Doesn't look like the same guy, does it? I could be all wrong about this creep, but after discovering him in that yearbook, my gut tells me he's involved somehow. So what would connect him to the girls other than he knew them."

Max stood quietly studying the picture, a curl of smoke circling his head. "That might be all it would take, plus, Destiny and Carmen are beautiful women." He rubbed a hand across his chin, then pointed at the mug shot. "You know, I've seen this guy before."

"You've probably spotted him here. From the rumors I've heard, he frequents the casinos and bingo halls. He sounds like a compulsive gambler. I want to find out more about him before I push too hard. When I approached him at White Oaks and asked about Destiny, he literally freaked out and left. I just hope my questions didn't scare him so much that he lies low. It will make it a lot harder to trace his activities. Especially, after the apartment manager told me he rarely showed up at his pad. Kinda strange for a man not to sleep at his own place."

"He might have a girlfriend. But if he's a gambler, he won't be able to stay away from the slots or tables for long. I'll keep an eye out and let you know. How can I reach you?"

Hawkman wrote a number on the back of one of his cards. "I've always got my cell phone with me. The only problem is, I'll have to stay out of his sight because he'll recognize me. But if you let me know he's here, I can wait in the parking lot. I know his truck."

"Sounds good." Max slipped the card into his pocket and crushed out his cigarette into the concrete ashtray provided at the doorway. "Gotta get back to work. I'll keep in touch."

Hawkman cashed in his fifty dollar jackpot then headed for the police station. He found Detective Williams hovering over a pile of paper. "Good Lord, man, don't you get writer's cramp from holding that pen for hours?"

Williams dropped it on the paper and flexed his hand. "I wake up in the middle of the night with my fingers bent and cramped. I have to manually pull them back into shape."

Hawkman scooted a chair up to the desk. "I can believe it."

"You sounded as if you had something interesting to tell me."

"I'd like to do more research on this guy and thought maybe you could help." Hawkman showed him the picture of Destiny and Tony at the prom, plus the one of Carmen in the yearbook. "These three people knew each other in the past. I'd like to look more into Tony Ricardo's years after high school and wondered if you knew anything about him or his family?"

"Oh, yeah, I told you I'd look up this guy and never got around to it. Let me do some digging and I'll get back to you tomorrow. The name doesn't ring any bells. But right now I'm tired and my brain's dead."

Hawkman stood and pushed the chair back against the wall. "Thanks. I'll get out of here so you can finish your work and get home to a good bed. I just worry as each day goes by and we haven't made any headway on Destiny's case. Every twenty-four hours the percentages drop for our finding her alive."

Williams took a deep breath and leaned back in his chair. "I know. I've got men working around the clock on both these women. It's worrisome. Not a trace of either. There's something screwy going on here and I don't like it. Maybe this lead on Tony Ricardo will amount to something. I sure hope so."

Hawkman gave a salute and headed out the door.

❧

"So what the hell are we going to do?"

"I don't know. Just, shut-up, dammit, and let me think. You keep blabbing and it interrupts my train of thought. For one thing, you gotta keep your cool. You go off the deep end and they'll suspect something sure as hell, if they don't already."

"Yeah, I know. But what do you expect me to do when that one-eyed Jack slams that picture in my face?"

"You sure as hell don't react like you did and try to run him down. Now, I suggest you get back to your usual gambling. You all of a sudden drop out of sight and the cops are gonna start looking for ya."

"Maybe I should apologize to that P.I. the next time I see him. I'll tell him I'd heard about Destiny disappearing, and it scared me when he started asking me questions."

The other man smirked. "Hmm, not a bad idea. That might just throw him off track enough to give us more time." He patted Tony on the back. "You got more brains than I thought."

"Thanks. I've had 'em all along, just don't use 'em much."

The man let out a mocking laugh. "Okay, I"m outta here. Get back to your vices so people know you ain't skipped out. Remember, you got nothin' to hide."

"Yeah, right."

The man had his hand on the doorknob then turned around. "On second thought, if that one-eyed fellow keeps giving you the run around, you might make sure you knock him down and roll over him next time." His mouth turned up in a wicked grin and he left, banging the door behind him.

Tony slumped down in one of the kitchen chairs and dropped his head onto his arms. After a few minutes, he got up, took a beer from the refrigerator and twisted off the top as he meandered into the living room. He slumped down onto the couch, turned the bottle up and took a gulp, then wiped his mouth with the back of his hand. "That bastard tells me I got nothin' to hide. Little does he know." He raised a curled fist toward the ceiling and shook it hard. "By damn, this better be worth it or there'll be hell to pay."

CHAPTER THIRTEEN

Before heading home, Hawkman swung by the White Oak Bingo Hall. The large building sat back off the road and housed more businesses than just the bingo parlor, which was located at the far end. The other offices were closed, but he couldn't see the entire parking lot because it circled around like a horse shoe. He took his time as he pulled into the entrance and checked the parked vehicles, searching for the Dodge truck before exiting behind the structure. Satisfied that Tony hadn't made it for the games that night, Hawkman left the area and headed home. About the time he hit the city limits, his cell phone vibrated against his waist.

He yanked it from his belt and put it to his ear. "Hello."

"Hawkman, Max."

"Yeah, what's up?"

"That guy, Tony Ricardo. He's here."

"Did he just arrive?"

"I think so. I've been patrolling the casino tonight and I just spotted him at the blackjack table. I'd have noticed him earlier."

"Great. I'm heading your way. I won't come inside because he'll recognize me. I'll find his truck and wait for him. Thanks, Max."

"You bet. Good luck."

Hawkman made a U-turn and headed back toward the Indian casino. He hoped he'd make it in time to catch Tony before he left. It puzzled him where this man spent his nights.

It took him about thirty minutes to reach the casino; then he searched the large maze of vehicles that stretched over two city blocks for Tony's truck. He finally spotted it in the second row facing the entrance. Finding a vacant spot several spaces behind the Dodge, he parked, pushed back the seat, adjusted his hat low over his eyes and waited.

⁂

Jennifer finished her dinner and cleaned up. With the Wilson case hanging over Hawkman's head, it didn't surprise her that he'd missed dinner. She fixed him a submarine sandwich out of the left-over tri-tip, wrapped it in foil and put it into the refrigerator, knowing he'd be famished when he arrived home.

She'd just sat down at the computer when the phone rang. Thinking it might be her husband, she figured she'd better answer instead of letting the machine pick up.

"Hello."

"Is this the one-eyed private investigator's woman?" A muffled voice asked.

A chill went down her back and she immediately punched on the recorder. "This is his wife."

"Well, tell that son-of-a-bitch that if he doesn't back off, the next one that disappears might be his pretty little wife."

"Who is this?"

The line went dead. Jennifer hung up, glad that she'd thought to start the recorder. She'd received threatening calls before when her husband had cases, so it didn't really bother her too much. However, just to be on the safe side, she went back to the bedroom, removed her fanny-pack gun holster from the dresser drawer and clipped it around her waist. Then she took her gun from the bedside table, loaded it, put on the safety and slid the pistol inside the pack.

Giving it a pat, she locked the doors, secured the windows and flipped on the alarm system. These were the precautions that Hawkman had instructed her to do any time a threatening call came in. He'd know she'd set the alarm by the blinking red light at the entry.

⁂

At midnight, Ricardo came out the front door of the casino. The way he kept glancing back gave Hawkman the impression the man may have won some money and wanted to make sure no one followed him outside. He watched him hurry to his truck and jump inside.

Hawkman waited until the Dodge pulled out of the parking section before he started his 4X4. The well-lit lot pretty much guaranteed that he wouldn't lose him. Keeping back a good distance, he followed Ricardo into town. It surprised Hawkman that the man headed straight for his apartment and pulled into his numbered parking slot. He recalled while hiding in that pantry, the man stayed only long enough to gather up a few kinky goodies before leaving. Deciding to give him some time, Hawkman parked on the street where he had full view of Ricardo's door.

A light came on inside the flat, then after a short time it went out. He waited in anticipation for the man to return to his truck. But after thirty minutes, and no sign of Ricardo, Hawkman hit the steering wheel with his fist. "Damn," he said aloud. "I would pick the night he decided to sleep in his own bed."

Reluctantly, Hawkman started the engine and pulled away from the curb. When he arrived home and started to insert his key into the front door, he spotted the tiny blinking red light above the alert slot and his heart squeezed. Something had happened to make Jennifer turn on the alarm. He pulled a small credit-like card from his wallet and pushed it into the opening, deactivating the system. When he entered the house, all his senses intensified to high alert.

Immediately, he headed back to the bedroom and found the lamp on with Jennifer sound asleep, an open book resting on her chest, her gun on the bedside table. He debated whether to wake her and find out what had made her activate the system or wait until morning. Studying her serene expression, he decided on the latter. Gently, he removed the book and placed it on the table, then switched off the light.

She made a slight moaning noise and rolled over, pulling the covers up over her shoulder. He smiled and thought how beautiful she looked with her long brown hair spread over the pillow, and a complexion so smooth it glowed in the dark. Thanking his lucky stars she belonged to him, he vowed to never let any thing happen to her, and climbed into bed.

The next morning Jennifer told him about the phone call and punched on the phone recorder.

Hawkman listened with interest, then rewound it several times. He shook his head. "The voice is muffled, like there's a towel over the receiver. But something about the inflection sure sounds familiar. I'm going to have to think about it." He flipped out the cartridge and replaced it with a new one. "I don't know what we're dealing with right now, so for the next few days keep the alarm on. And keep vigilant if you're outside. In fact, carry your gun."

She nodded. "I have the impression that Destiny's case is more dangerous than you suspected."

"It seems to be heading in that direction, especially with this call. I don't want you to take any chances, so notify me immediately if you spot anyone following you or any suspicious characters around the house. Right now we haven't a clue who's involved in this, but we're examining the possibility that it could be connected to another missing woman. I'm going to take this recording to Williams and see what he thinks."

"Another missing woman? Who?" Jennifer asked, wide-eyed.

"Carmen Pritchard."

"But that happened several weeks ago. I remember reading about it in the paper. You think they're connected?"

"There are a lot of similarities in the two cases. Neither of their cars have been found and no bodies discovered. It's like they vanished into thin air. I want you to be extremely careful."

"That is weird. Do you think there's a possibility that they're still alive?"

Hawkman shrugged. "Anything's possible. But it worries me as each day goes by without a clue." He glanced up at her. "By the way, are you free tonight?"

"Sure. Why do you ask?"

"I need you to go to bingo."

CHAPTER FOURTEEN

When Jennifer entered the White Oak Bingo Hall, she headed toward the table where her friends, Patty, Rita and Pat Kay were all sitting.

But before she reached them, Argy stepped in front of her, his glasses swinging from one ear. He glanced at the door. "Where's your scary husband? Is he investigating us today?" Turning to another customer, he pointed at Jennifer. "You know her husband? He's a private investigator and looks for murderers. And she writes about murderers, kills off everyone in her books." He then glanced back at her. "Isn't that right, Ms. Murderer?"

Jennifer laughed. "That's correct and you're going to be a character in my next novel."

Argy grinned and held up a stack of flash boards. "You want to buy some of these?"

"Maybe later," she said, shaking her head as she scooted around him and headed toward her friends. "Hi, gals. Is there room for me?"

"Sure," Patty said. "Both tables are reserved for us, so there's plenty of space."

She sat down and surveyed the crowd.

Rita glanced up from opening a handful of flash boards. "Didn't you bring your books? I wanted to buy one for a friend."

"They're in the car. I can get what you want at the break."

Pat Kay, the retired school teacher, touched Jennifer's arm and pointed toward the cashier. "You better get in line before it gets too long. You want to have time to get the homework done."

"I know, I'm running late and my mind is elsewhere," Jennifer said, digging her billfold from her purse.

"Try to relax," Patty said. "Get your mind off mystery plotting. You need a mental break."

"You're absolutely right. But I can't get Hawkman's case off my mind. And it's the real thing."

"Is it about Destiny Wilson?" Rita asked.

"That's the one," Jennifer said, as she left the table and rushed toward the forming line.

A few minutes later, she hurried back to the table with two bingo machines and a raft of papers, plus a handful of flash boards. She plopped down at the end of the table facing the aisle, took a deep breath, set up her machines and stacked her papers in the proper order.

Patty leaned forward and whispered. "Does Hawkman suspect someone who plays bingo?"

Jennifer shrugged. "He's working with the police and they're mostly checking out leads right now."

The women spent a few silent moments preparing their papers for the games. Jennifer thought about Hawkman circling the parking lot waiting for her call. So far, she hadn't spotted Tony or any other suspicious characters entering the hall. Fred, Argy's brother, appeared at her side.

"Hello, you want some flashes? I love this game."

She smiled. "Fred, you and that brother of yours are silver-tongued foxes. You can talk people into spending money as if it grew on a tree in their backyards."

He threw back his head and laughed.

She handed him a ten dollar bill. "You better give me a winner."

Fred continued down the aisle giving Jennifer time to finish daubing her papers. Suddenly, she had that eerie feeling of being watched. When she glanced up, her heart thumped. Tony Ricardo stood in the doorway, his stare boring into her like a sharp knife. When she met his gaze, he immediately headed for the purchase line.

Rita touched her shoulder. "You okay? Your face is ashen, like you've just seen a ghost."

Jennifer sucked in her breath and grabbed her purse. "I'll be right back."

She left the room, went outside and punched in Hawkman's number. "I hope you're close. We're about to start and Tony's here."

"Yeah, I'm almost there, but where are you? I don't hear any noise."

"I'm out on the patio. I don't get as much static."

"Get the hell back into the hall and don't go outside alone again."

Taken aback by his tone of voice, she hesitated. "Why are you talking to me like that? Surely he's not that dangerous."

"Don't forget the phone call you received. Stay on your toes!"

A tinge of fear slid down her spine and she frantically glanced around before dashing inside. "I forgot about that. I'm back in the building."

"Good. Don't leave for home tonight until I tell you it's safe."

"Okay," she said, gnawing her lower lip as she crossed the room toward the table.

❦

After Jennifer abruptly left the room, Patty whispered to the other two ladies. "There's something going on. Did you see that frightened look on her face when Tony walked in?"

"Yes," Rita said. "I asked if she felt all right."

Pat Kay nodded. "That guy would scare the devil. Do you think he might have had something to do with Destiny's disappearance?"

About that time, Tony walked by their table and the women's gaze followed him as he moved toward the front entry.

"We can't let him go outside," Pat Kay whispered harshly, "Jennifer's out there alone." She leaped from her seat and grabbed one of her papers. "Oh, Tony," she called, waving the sheet. "Check your Double Actions and see if you have them all. I think you might have dropped one."

He jerked around in surprise. "Uh, I don't think so, but I'll go and look." Pat Kay followed him back to his table. He counted out his papers and shook his head. "No, they're all here."

When she spotted Jennifer coming back into the hall, she shrugged and turned back toward her table. "Oh well, I found it on the floor after you walked by. Thought it might be yours."

"Yeah, thanks," he said, with a note of disgust in his voice.

Jennifer collapsed into her seat and clipped the phone onto the waistband of her jeans just as Ed sat down at the caller's chair.

"Could we have it a little quieter, please? It's awfully hard to hear with this machine going. Before we start the session, we'll be playing Keno, Double Dab and Rapid." He thumped the microphone on his hand. "Would you people please be quiet!"

"Oh, dear, he doesn't sound in a very good mood tonight," Patty said.

Jennifer grinned. "I think he's due for a trip back to Minnesota."

Rita chuckled and nodded. "It does tend to help."

❧

Meanwhile, Hawkman swung into the parking lot and made the circle. When he found the green Dodge, he parked several spaces away in a darkened area. He walked around to the front of the bingo hall and peered into the window covered with a glaze that allowed him to see in, but no one could see out. Almost as good as a two-way mirror, he thought.

He spotted Tony near the back of the hall and also noted Jennifer with her clan of friends busily daubing away at their papers. The games were in full swing and he figured he had a good forty-five minutes before the first break.

Hawkman scurried back to Tony's truck and glanced inside. He didn't see any alarm signal blinking, although he knew they were installed on these models. Luckily it hadn't been set. He quickly removed the small pick tool from his pocket and worked it into the key slot. Within a few minutes he had the door unlocked and the dome light disabled. He then slid into the seat of the Dodge.

Taking the small flashlight he carried on his keyring, he swept the beam across the floorboard and found it cluttered with napkins, fast food sacks and roach clips. He felt under the seats and discovered a bag of marijuana. This would give Williams a good excuse to stop the truck if they needed to nab Tony, so he tossed it back into its hiding place. Flipping open the glove compartment, he shuffled through the items and found a folded sheet of paper under the owner's manual. It appeared to be a hand-sketched map. Shoving it into his pocket, he tossed the manual back into the glove compartment and closed the cubby hole.

At that moment, he heard voices and glanced up to see a couple of women strolling along the back of the building. The early bird session had gone faster than he'd expected. He slipped out of the cab, locked the door from the inside and gently pushed it shut.

Staying in the shadows, Hawkman snuck back to his own vehicle. Inside, he took a mini-light he kept in the truck and tried to decipher the hand-drawn sketch. It didn't make much sense, so he tucked it back into his pocket and decided to wait until he got home where he could study it under better light.

He hated to call Jennifer on the cell phone, remembering that the first time they'd gone to bingo, a short gal with a cropped curly hairdo, sitting in the back of the room yelled, 'HELLO', every time a phone rang with its cute little jingle. Needless to say, that would embarrass Jennifer and she would definitely let him know about it later. But he needed to leave since a security guard had driven through earlier and noticed him sitting in his truck. He didn't want to be parked here when the guy made his next round. Hoping Jennifer had her phone handy, he punched the memory button.

"Hello," she whispered.

"Sorry, I had to call you in the middle of a game. Hope it didn't disturb anyone."

"No, I had it on vibrate on my waist. What do you want?"

"I have to get out of the parking lot. There's a security guard making rounds and he's already spotted me once. As soon as bingo's over, call me."

"Okay, bye."

Hawkman, clipped the phone back on his belt and started the 4X4. As he pulled out of the exit onto the street, he spotted the security's white vehicle turning into the entrance. He could have explained his presence; he just didn't want to take the time. Glancing at the clock on the dashboard, he read nine-thirty. It would be forty-five minutes to an hour before bingo finished. Not having eaten since breakfast, he searched for a fast-food place. When he spotted a Burger King, he pulled into the drive-thru and ordered a hamburger and fries. Gulping down the sandwich, Hawkman glanced at his gas gauge and noticed he had less than a quarter of a tank.

"Damn," he said aloud. "I've got to get fuel before I can tail Ricardo."

He drove up and down the streets until he finally found an open station. While waiting for the attendant to fill the tank, he felt the cell phone vibrate against his hip. He yanked it off and put it to his ear.

"Yeah?"

"Bingo's finished, and Tony just left out the back door."

"Okay, thanks."

Hawkman paid the attendant in cash, hit the accelerator and raced down the street. Fortunately, he hadn't driven more than a few blocks and came in sight of the building just as the green Dodge exited the parking lot.

"Damn," he muttered. "I wanted to talk to that slime ball before he left."

The Dodge turned in the opposite direction, forcing Hawkman to quickly pull into a driveway and back up. He hung behind a couple of cars to avoid being spotted by Ricardo. This time, Tony didn't head in the direction of his apartment, but drove south toward the hills.

CHAPTER FIFTEEN

Hawkman kept Ricardo's truck in sight although there were two vehicles between them. He thought it odd when he noticed the Dodge's right turn signal come on. The off ramp coming up led to a road going into the hills, which turned into gravel about five miles out. Why would Ricardo exit there?

As the Dodge turned off, the brake lights of the vehicle directly behind him popped on bright and clear, then veered to the left. But the mini-van driver in front of Hawkman, slammed on his brakes and laid rubber along the highway as he fish-tailed for several feet. The van then skidded into the shallow right ditch and bounced to a stop.

Hawkman checked his rearview mirror and pulled into the left lane barely missing the big three point buck deer that had slid off the van's hood. Parking on the side of the road, Hawkman jumped out and dialed 911 on his cell phone as he raced toward the damaged vehicle. Just as he reached the driver's side, a man climbed out and pushed open the side panel door, while a woman in the passenger seat did the same. Two children about ten and fourteen bounced out.

"Dad, what happened?" they questioned in unison.

"Is everyone okay?" Hawkman asked.

The man glanced at his wife and she nodded. "Yes, I think we're fine. Maybe a bit in shock." He wiped a hand across his forehead. "I couldn't figure out why that car ahead suddenly swerved. Then I saw the deer and couldn't stop in time."

"They jump out on the highway and become hypnotized by car lights. And it's hard to see them at night because of their coloring." Hawkman walked to the front of the van, noting the mashed grill where water and antifreeze gushed from the radiator, making a large puddle on the ground. Also a headlight dangled over the bumper, hanging by its wires. "Looks like your vehicle is badly damaged. You won't be able to drive it. I've called for help and they should arrive pretty soon."

The man held out his hand. "Thank you so much for stopping. Really appreciate it. My name's Charles Hill, this is my wife, Kristy, and these are our two kids, Jane and Phil."

Hawkman shook his hand. "Tom Casey. Glad no one got hurt." He turned toward the road and pointed. "While we're waiting for help, I'm going to pull that deer off the highway before someone else gets into trouble."

"I'll give you a hand," Charles said, and the two men headed toward the dead animal. Once they got it to the side of the road, Mr. Hill put his fists on his hips and stared down at the stag. "What a beautiful animal. Such a shame."

Hawkman patted him on the shoulder. "Just be thankful you and your family didn't get hurt. I've seen accidents involving deer that would make your stomach turn."

Within a few minutes two patrol cars, an ambulance and a tow truck, with their lights and sirens blaring, rolled to the scene. After a quick check of the Hill family by the paramedics, the ambulance left, and the police proceeded to take measurements of the skid marks. Then they called Fish and Game to bring a vehicle large enough to remove the animal carcass.

When the tow driver had the van loaded, the family scrambled into one of the patrol cars. They all turned and waved at Hawkman as they drove off behind the truck carrying their mangled vehicle.

Soon, the highway looked as if nothing had happened. Hawkman climbed into his 4X4 and headed down the off ramp where he'd seen the Dodge disappear. He surveyed both sides of the road until it turned into gravel. Seeing no vehicles or signs of life, he did a U-turn and decided to make a daylight run into this area tomorrow.

The next morning, Hawkman arose early, grabbed his clothes and tiptoed out of the bedroom, softly closing the door so Jennifer could sleep. He called Detective Williams' office and it didn't surprise him to hear the man answer. "Did you go home last night or sleep in your chair?"

The detective laughed. "Would you believe a little of both."

"Yeah, I believe it."

"Funny you should call. I had one of my men do a background search on Tony Ricardo. He gave me the report last night. It's too long to read over the phone. Want to drop by and look it over?"

"Yeah, this guy has piqued my interest. Also, I've got a tape of a threatening phone call Jennifer received that I want you to hear. Will you be there in a couple of hours?"

"Yep, unless a riot breaks out downtown."

Hawkman chuckled. "Any motorcycle rallies in the area?"

"God, I hope not, but that might make for some excitement around here. Oh, by the way, heard you reported that accident last night where that guy collided with a big buck."

"Yeah. It could have been worse. The first car missed him by veering to the left. But the poor guy in front of me didn't see the deer in time and ended up with the stag on his hood. Fortunately, no one got hurt, just a battered front-end of a mini-van."

"Lucky folks. What were you doing in that area?"

"I'll tell you when I get there."

"Okay, see ya shortly."

After hanging up, Hawkman took the phone book from the shelf and looked up the doctor's name he'd seen on the medications in Ricardo's medicine cabinet. He found a Dr. Crowley, M.D., listed in a small square that advertised 'Private Practice'. It stated the doctor had served the area for thirty years. Odd, he'd never heard of him. That could be good or bad. Fortunately, he and Jennifer had a health plan that supplied their own doctors and they didn't have to worry about searching for one.

Hawkman jotted down the information and stuck it in his pocket. He then went into the kitchen where he noticed Jennifer had a package of breakfast rolls thawing on the counter. But when he spotted, 'low-fat', 'sugar-free' pastries printed across the top, he wrinkled his nose. Grumbling, he poured a cup of coffee and had a bowl of dry cereal instead.

He wrote Jennifer a quick note, telling her he'd left early to work on Destiny's case. Plopping on his hat, he pulled on his jeans jacket and patted its pocket to make sure he had the recording. When he stepped outside, he hesitated for only a moment before pushing the card into the slot and activating the alarm. Better to be safe than sorry, he thought, climbing into his truck.

Reaching the city limits of Medford, he headed straight for the police station and parked in the visitors' lot. Maybe the Ricardo report would give him extra information to discuss with the doctor. He also figured he'd make a run by Barney & Baker's law offices and ask Rene about Tony Ricardo. Since this whole group went to the same high school, maybe she could shed a little more light on the relationship of the three.

As Hawkman rounded the corner of the hallway toward Williams' office, he heard the unmistakable sound of an electric razor. He poked his head around the door jamb and chuckled. The detective was signing papers with his right hand while running an electric razor over the day old stubble on his chin with his left. "Hey, you can do two things at once. We men aren't supposed to be able to do that."

Williams laughed. "In this business we don't follow the norm. You ought to know that by now." He flipped off the shaver, hit it a couple of times on the edge of the plastic wastebasket, then placed it in a side drawer. Removing a stapled set of papers from underneath the pile on his desk, he handed them to Hawkman. "Think you'll find this report on Tony Ricardo mighty interesting. I made an extra copy, so you can keep this one. I'm tempted to pull this guy in and question him myself."

Hawkman raised his brows. "Really! That bad, huh?"

"It's mighty suspicious how his parents died. In fact, this guy is surrounded by deaths."

"I suspect he's of questionable character," Hawkman said, rolling the papers into a tube and sticking them into his pocket. "I followed him last night and he took that off ramp leading into the hills. But, I got detained due to the accident and never did find out where he went." He tossed the hand-sketched map he'd found in Tony's truck onto the desk. "Can you decipher this? You're more familiar with that area than I am. Maybe it will make some sense to you."

"Williams studied the piece of paper, turning it around in his hand. "Where'd you get this?"

"That's immaterial."

He gave Hawkman a knowing look. "It appears to be a map, but you can't tell which is north or south."

"Yeah, I agree. Just hoped that maybe you might recognize some of the lines that resemble roads or streets."

The detective shook his head. "Right off the top of my head I can't help you. Sorry." He handed it back. "Now, what's this threatening call to Jennifer that you mentioned?"

Hawkman pulled the cassette from his pocket and handed it to him. The detective reached into the bottom drawer of his desk and took out a small recorder. He clicked the tape into place and turned it on. They both listened intently.

Williams frowned. "Sounds like a male voice with a rag over the mouthpiece." He glanced at Hawkman. "You have any idea who it is?"

"Something about the inflections in that voice makes me think I've heard it before. Right now I can't pinpoint where in my mind. But Ricardo is definitely a possibility. Maybe in a couple of days I'll have an answer."

"Let me know what you come up with. We need every clue we can get."

About that time, the phone jangled on William's desk.

Hawkman shoved the tape back into his pocket and stood. "Thanks for the copy of the report. I'll read it in my truck and get back to you later if I have any questions." He waved and headed out of the office.

Climbing into his SUV, he left the door open to let the heat escape and sat sideways on the seat, his feet resting on the running board. He pushed back his hat with his finger and unrolled the report. His elbows perched on his knees, he turned the pages and his jaw tightened. Taking a toothpick from his jeans jacket pocket, he stuck it between his teeth and chewed on the end. He slowly folded the papers as he stared out across the parking lot. He wondered how Dr. Crowley would explain his prescribing medications to dead people.

Shifting his legs into the cab, he slammed the door and stuck the data into Destiny's folder. He'd learned from experience to keep the file of his current case with him at all times, rather than take the chance of someone ransacking his office and stealing them.

Hawkman drove to the address he'd found in the phone book. It surprised him to find the office in a residential area. But a shingle over the front door, reading "Dr. Crowley, M.D." verified he'd come to the right place. Tossing his toothpick into the ashtray, he climbed out of the 4X4 and strolled toward the entry. A small sign attached over the doorbell instructed one to come in.

Hawkman slowly opened the door and peered into a waiting room with a couple of people sitting in overstuffed chairs reading magazines. At the far end, a young Asian woman sat at a desk in front of a hallway. Her long black hair hung to her waist and moved slightly as she typed on the computer. Hawkman assumed the area behind her led to the examination rooms. As he approached the desk, she glanced up.

"Hello sir. May I have your name and time of appointment?"

"I don't have one, but would like to speak to Dr. Crowley on a business matter."

She wrinkled her forehead. "What type of business?"

His back to the waiting patients, he discreetly flashed his

badge and quickly returned it to his pocket. "Does he have an opening today?"

Gnawing her lip, she fidgeted with her pencil, and quickly dragged a chart toward her. Looking up with big brown eyes, she asked in a quavering voice. "Could you return in an hour? He'll be through with his patients by then."

Hawkman noted her name tag, Elaine Chen. "Thank you, Ms. Chen. I'll be back." He turned to leave.

"Wait, sir," she said, half rising from her chair. "May I have your name, please?"

"Sure." Instead of blurting out that he was a private investigator, Hawkman handed her one of his business cards.

After reading it, she looked on the verge of tears. "Thank you," she said, clipping it to a holder on the computer.

Hawkman drove away wondering why he'd made the receptionist so nervous. Did she have something to hide? The thought soon left him as he worried that it had been almost a week since Destiny had disappeared, and he didn't feel any closer to finding out what had happened. Yet, in his gut he felt he was on the right track. He checked his watch and planned to return to the doctor's office at three o'clock sharp.

CHAPTER SIXTEEN

An hour only gave Hawkman enough time to grab a quick bite. He pulled into a drive-thru, ordered a cheeseburger, fries and tall soda, then parked in the lot to eat. He didn't realize his need for nourishment until the aroma circled his nose, causing his stomach to growl. Shifting the seat back as far as it would go, he got comfortable and unwrapped the sandwich, folding a napkin around the underneath half to catch any juices that might drip on his clothes. He munched on the fries between bites of the burger and smiled to himself when he thought this might not be the best food for a body, but it sure tasted good.

Halfway through the meal, he reached down and took the Ricardo report from the file. Both of Tony's parents had died on the same night in their sleep, appearing as a murder-suicide. Tony had been questioned and came up with a witness, a hooker from a neighboring town, who swore that he'd spent the night in question at her place. Two weeks later, the authorities discovered her body in a car at the bottom of a nearby ravine. She'd been dead over a week.

After a brief investigation, the police closed the case and listed it as an ordinary solo automobile accident. Hawkman questioned the handling of this suspicious action. With the advances in forensics and possible clues that could could have been found, it didn't make sense.

He stared out the window for a few moments, then glanced back down at the report and noted that all the deaths occurred within the past year. The dates on the medications he'd spotted in Ricardo's apartment were no more than six months old. This is mighty strange, he thought. He had good cause to question Dr. Crowley and his post mortem prescriptions.

Hawkman finished eating and tossed the debris in the parking lot waste container. Climbing back into the 4X4, he checked his watch and figured Dr. Crowley should be finished with his last patient by now.

Parking on the street in front of the residential office, he noted that the two cars formerly parked in the driveway had disappeared. He strolled into the empty waiting room and found Ms. Chen still at her station, dressed in a white lab coat and working diligently at the computer. She glanced up, gave him a faint smile and stood.

"Dr. Crowley will see you now. Please come this way."

Detouring around the desk, Hawkman followed her down the hallway to the end room where she tapped lightly on a closed door that had 'Office' posted across the center.

"Yes."

She opened it a few inches and poked her head inside. "Mr. Casey is here."

"Show him in."

She stepped aside and motioned for Hawkman to enter. "May I leave now?" she asked her boss.

"Yes, Ms. Chen, Have a good evening."

She nodded and left the room.

When Hawkman stepped into the immaculately clean office, the sight of the youthful man behind the desk took him by surprise.

The doctor rose and outstretched his hand. "Hello, Mr. Casey. How can I help you?"

"Excuse me for being taken aback," Hawkman said, as they shook. "But you don't look like you've been in practice for thirty years."

The young man laughed. "You're not the first who noticed." He motioned toward the chair in front of the desk. "Have a seat." As he settled in the swivel chair, he continued. "I took over my father's practice after he became ill."

"I see," Hawkman said. "How long ago would that be?"

The doctor scratched his head. "About five months."

"Hmm, you might not be able to help me. I think I'd better talk to your father. I'm afraid the questions I need answered took place before you arrived on the scene."

His smile turned somber. "Unfortunately, my father is in an Alzheimer's medical facility and I doubt he'll be of much help."

Hawkman felt the muscles in his neck tighten. "I'm assuming you have access to your father's files since you've taken over his patients."

"Yes, of course, but they're all confidential."

"I realize that. But I'm working on a case and discovered that some strong pain and sleeping medications have been frequently prescribed to two dead people."

The young man's eyes widened. "Could you give me the names of those individuals?"

"Yes, Elsa and Marco Ricardo."

Hawkman would have sworn he detected a glimmer of fear sweep across the man's face as he stood and crossed to a filing cabinet sitting in the far corner of the room. He rummaged through the drawers for several seconds, then pulled out two large folders and carried them back to his desk. Slipping on a pair of metal rimmed reading glasses, he thumbed through one file, then the other.

His face turned ashen as he read, then he closed the folder and glanced up. "Mr. Casey, I can't talk to you about these two people without first conferring with my lawyer. My father did some irrational things in his last few months of practice. I'll have to give you a call."

Hawkman handed him his card. "I'd appreciate any information as soon as possible."

❧

After Hawkman left the office, he headed for the police station. He knew from the look on the young doctor's face, that the only way he'd be able to look through those files was with a subpoena in hand. And for that, he needed Williams.

He didn't find the detective in his office. A cold cup of coffee sat on the corner of the desk and the missing jacket from the back of his chair indicated that he might be in the interrogation area or out on a case. Hawkman strolled down to the reception center. "Is Detective Williams in the building?" he asked the young woman at the desk.

She ran her finger down a sheet of paper. "No, he's been called out and I have no idea when he'll be back. Can I give him a message?"

Hawkman grimaced. "No, that's okay. I'll check back later. Thanks."

He glanced at his watch and discovered it was only four thirty. If he could catch Rene still at work, he wouldn't have to bother her at home. Maybe she could fill in a few gaps where he needed answers.

When Hawkman walked into the empty alcove of the lawyer's office where clients normally waited, Rene wasn't at her desk. A loud conversation echoed from the room located at the end of a short hallway off to his right. One of the voices sounded like Rene's. She soon stormed out of the opened door with a folder in her hand and smiled at Hawkman when she entered the reception area.

"My goodness, what brings you here at this late hour?"

"You didn't just get fired, did you?"

She threw back her head and laughed. "Oh, no. Old Mr. Smith is in there and he's deaf as a mole is blind. Flat refuses to wear a hearing aid, so all of us have to yell to make him understand what we're saying."

Hawkman wiped his forehead in fake motion. "Thank goodness. I figured I'd come at a bad time."

"Not at all." Then she frowned. "Do you have news about Destiny?"

He shook his head. "Nothing. I wish I did have something to tell you. But I wanted to ask if you knew Tony Ricardo?"

She had moved toward the filing cabinet, but stopped in her tracks. "Yes, I know him. Why? Do you think he had something to do with Destiny's disappearance?"

"I'm checking every avenue. Right now I have no suspects."

"Tony's a real pain in the butt," she said, putting the file away. Sitting at her desk, she motioned for Hawkman to take the chair in front of her. "Pardon my expression. But, he really is."

"What do you mean?" Hawkman asked, as he sat down.

"He always wants to join us girls at bingo and he stinks." She shook her head, a look of disgust on her face. "I don't know when that man bathes."

"Besides his personal hygiene, what else can you tell me about him?"

The corners of her mouth pulled down in disgust. "He's worthless."

"I've gathered that from what I've found out so far. Tell me about his folks."

Her chest heaved as she let out an audible sigh. "Those poor things. They died of an overdose of their medications. Makes me wonder if they didn't plan it that way. They were both terminally ill."

He nodded. "Where did they live?"

She gestured with a flip of her hand. "I don't rightly know, except out in the country somewhere. But Tony brought them into town to live so he could keep an eye on their well-being. How much good that did, I couldn't tell you. He took them out of their familiar surroundings and I'm not sure that's the best thing for old folks. They tend to go down-hill faster."

"You have any idea in which direction they used to live?"

She shook her head. "Sorry, I haven't the foggiest notion. But you could probably find out at the court house. I don't ever recall seeing in the paper where their property went up for sale after they died. I'd imagine it's either in Tony's name or still in his folks. They lived there for years before he moved them into town."

"Did you know Carmen Pritchard?"

"Oh yeah. We all went to school together. I haven't seen her in ages." Then Rene put a forefinger in the air. "Wait a minute.

I read in the paper a few weeks ago that she'd disappeared and the police were asking for help." Her eyes widened. "Dear God, do you think Destiny's and Carmen's disappearance are connected?"

"Not sure. But there's always that possibility."

"Carmen was a strange one in high school. Beautiful, but weird."

"What do you mean by 'weird'?"

"A girl with her good looks and figure could have had her pick of dates. Instead she chose the losers. We couldn't quite understand it. She didn't have the best reputation in the world, but it still befuddled us all."

Hawkman stood. "Thank you, Rene. This information helps."

Her expression solemn, she glanced up. "I keep thinking about Destiny winning blackout on B-13. It sends shivers down my spine. Do you think there's any hope of finding her alive?"

He tapped his fist on the desktop. "Never give up hope, Rene. Never."

A faint smile creased her lips. "I won't, Hawkman. I promise."

"Good. I'll let you know when we find her."

He left the lawyer's office. Knowing it was too late to go by the court house, he drove back to the police station. When he entered the building, he saw Detective Williams standing off to the side talking with some of his colleagues. He spotted Hawkman and called out. "Meet you in my office in a few seconds."

Hawkman waved and headed down the hallway. He helped himself to a cup of thick black coffee and sipped on it cautiously. Several minutes passed before Williams entered.

"Sorry about the delay, but had to give some instructions."

"No problem," Hawkman said.

"So what's on your mind at this late hour?"

"I went by Dr. Crowley's office to see the files on Tony Ricardo's parents. He won't show them to me until after he talks to his lawyer, and you know what that means. I'm going to need a subpoena."

The detective furrowed his brows. "I thought Dr. Crowley retired."

"His son has taken over the practice. Elsa and Marco Ricardo were patients of the older Dr. Crowley. His son told me that his dad has Alzheimer's and couldn't answer my questions."

"So, why do you want to see those files?"

"It appears that some pretty potent medications were prescribed for the older Ricardo's after they were deceased."

The detective raised a brow. "How did you find that out?"

Hawkman shifted in his seat. "Don't think you want to know."

Williams raked a hand across his forehead, pushing strands of hair back into place. "This definitely sounds like a can of worms. You think Tony's a pusher or an addict?"

"Not sure. Need to find out a few more things." Hawkman leaned his elbow on the desk. "By the way, do you know where the Ricardos lived before Tony moved them into town?"

Williams shook his head. "No. I'd never heard of these people until you brought them to my attention. You could check at the court house."

"Yeah, I think I'll run over there Monday morning."

"We've got this Tony guy under suspicion, so shouldn't have any trouble getting a subpoena for those medical files. I'll get on it first thing. Check back here tomorrow afternoon."

"Thanks. See ya then," Hawkman said, leaving the detective's office.

As he climbed into the cab of the 4X4, he felt his phone vibrate against his waist. "Hello."

"Hawkman, Jennifer. Just had a phone call routed from your office. Teley from the bingo hall wants you to come by. He said one of the players asked to talk to you about Tony."

"That's strange. How would anyone know I have him under investigation?"

"Word passes fast among the bingo crowd and many

come to their own conclusions about certain things. And they desperately want to help find Destiny."

"Well, who knows, maybe it'll pay off." He adjusted his seat belt and put the key into the ignition.

"I'll put your dinner in the refrigerator. You can zap it in the microwave when you get home."

He chuckled. "Thanks, hon. Talk to you later."

When Hawkman reached the White Oaks Hall, bingo had started.

CHAPTER SEVENTEEN

Hawkman entered the bingo hall and quietly crossed the room toward the office area. He couldn't help chuckling when he heard the loud voice of Argy selling flash boards. "Raise your hand, not your finger." the man bellowed.

Poking his head inside the open window, Hawkman got the manager's attention. "Jennifer tells me you have a customer who wants to talk to me."

"Yeah, but you might want to wait until after bingo," Teley said in a low voice, then nodded toward the large room. "Tony's here."

Hawkman casually surveyed the area and spotted Ricardo sitting at a back table near the wall with his head down concentrating on the papers in front of him. He turned back to Teley. "Does everyone know that I have Tony under suspicion?"

A tight grin curled the corners of Teley's mouth. "Seems like bingo people do a lot of gossiping among themselves. We've even had a few incidents with Tony since the disappearance of Destiny."

"Anything you'd like to tell me about?"

"Not sure it'll help."

"I'll sort it out."

"Okay, I'll talk to you outside at the break."

"Who's the customer that wants to speak to me?"

Teley, still keeping his voice low, pointed toward the center of the room. "See the two black women seated in the third row at the table near the aisle? The younger one has her hair done in French braids."

Hawkman glanced in that direction and nodded. "Yeah."

"They're mother and daughter. The daughter's name is Teresa, and the mother's is Grace."

"So which one wants to talk to me?"

"Not sure. They were together when they asked if you'd be here tonight. I told them I didn't know, but that I could certainly contact you if they felt it necessary. They thought it important, so I put a call into your office and reached Jennifer. You know the rest."

"I appreciate it." Hawkman stepped aside as a late comer waited patiently behind him. "I'll see you in the parking lot."

As he headed toward the door, Hawkman glanced back at Ricardo and felt the man's acid stare bore into him.

Strolling up and down in front of the hall, Hawkman spotted the parked green Dodge and noticed dirt splattered on its sides, along with clumps of dried soil hanging on the inside fender walls. It had rained the night before and that truck had been somewhere on an unpaved road. No way could he have gotten that kind of mud driving on a concrete or asphalt surface. He decided to thoroughly explore that region where he'd seen Tony exit off the freeway when the deer accident happened.

People soon filed out the door to get a breath of fresh air, Ricardo among them. Seemed like more players came outside than stayed in the building, Hawkman thought, as he watched them meander around on the patio. He soon spotted the manager peering over the heads of the crowd. Hawkman waved, and Teley stepped off a concrete curb surrounding a flower box and wove his way through the bodies.

"Man, it does get smoky in there," he said, shaking his head. "Guess it fits with the gambling trend."

Hawkman grinned as they walked away from the crowd, leaving Ricardo staring after them.

The manager shook his head. "I'm surprised to see Tony here after the episode the other night."

"Tell me what happened?"

"Elvis asked Tony where that pretty little Destiny had gone."

Hawkman raised a brow. "How did he react to that question?"

Teley shook his head. "The man practically came unglued. He jumped out of his seat, grabbed Elvis by the shirt and wanted to know if that private investigator had been nosing around again."

"Oh, hell," Hawkman said, throwing his hands up in despair. "Nothing like my presence causing a problem at your bingo games. I'm really sorry."

Teley smirked. "Hey, don't worry about it. Elvis handled it very efficiently. He yanked Tony's hands away, shoved him back into his seat, and told him never to grab him like that again. My workers may seem like mild and funny men, but you don't want to mess with them like that. They won't stand for it."

Hawkman thought of the worker's physiques. "I believe it. They're all very athletic in appearance."

"They've been through rougher ordeals in their lives than that little display with Tony. They keep in shape and are definitely not wimps."

Hawkman kept his eye on Ricardo as the two men talked. Soon, Tony went back inside and Grace approached. "Excuse me, Mr. Casey. I'm assuming Teley told you my daughter wants a word with you. When would be a good time?"

The manager turned toward her. "I suggested that you wait until after bingo and let Tony get out of here so you won't be seen speaking to the private investigator."

"I'll stay outside until I'm sure he's gone," Hawkman said. "Then I'll come in and we can talk."

Grace nodded. "That's a good idea. I'll tell my daughter and we'll see you later." She headed toward the door and joined a group of women going back into the hall.

After a few minutes, Hawkman stood alone in the parking lot and knew he had at least an hour and a half before the games were over. He headed for his truck, remembering he'd seen a Togo's Sandwich place down the road. His stomach growled in anticipation.

He drove back to the bingo hall and found a parking spot

where he could keep an eye on the Dodge as he munched his pastrami sandwich.

Soon, people were leaving, chatting loudly as they headed for their cars. Tony came out and calmly marched straight toward his truck. He drove past the 4X4 without even giving it a second glance. This nagged at Hawkman. The man seemed lacking in scruples and fear. He wished he could follow him, but the women were waiting.

After a few moments, assured that Ricardo didn't just circle the parking area, Hawkman left his truck and entered the near empty hall. Teresa and Grace sat at the table where they'd played, their bingo paraphernalia stored in bags on the chairs beside them. Grace held her daughter's trembling hands.

He approached the two women and slipped into a chair on the opposite side. "Good evening, ladies, I hope you had a winning night," he said, smiling.

Grace laughed. "We've definitely seen better times."

"I won't keep you long," Hawkman said, removing his recorder from his pocket and placing it on the table. "Hope you don't mind if I record our conversation, it's a lot more accurate than taking notes."

Teresa looked a little uncomfortable, but her mother said, "That's a great idea. Then you don't make any mistakes about what you've heard."

Hawkman nodded. "Exactly. Okay, say your names first, then tell me about Tony Ricardo."

After the women went through the preliminaries, Grace nudged Teresa. "Now, tell him about Mira."

"Who's Mira?" Hawkman asked.

The young woman cleared her throat. "Mira Jones. She's a friend of mine who got stranded at her job yesterday, so I gave her a ride home. We talked about Destiny's disappearance and wondered if Tony had anything to do with it. That's when she told me what he'd said."

Hawkman studied the woman's wide-eyed expression and sensed her uneasiness in repeating the conversation she'd had with her friend. "Don't be nervous, Teresa. Go on."

"I know this is hearsay," she said, clasping and unclasping her hands. "But I just thought it important."

"Please tell me what your friend heard."

"She'd been to the Triple 'C' and saw Tony. He'd sat beside her at one of the slots and talked about Destiny. Mira said he was drunk and really had a loose tongue."

"Go on."

"He told her he didn't understand why the big deal about Destiny because she was alive and well. Mira asked him how he could justify that statement. He told her to trust him, he knew it for a fact."

"That's very interesting. Where can I reach your friend, Mira? I'd like to speak with her."

She wiped a hand across her face. "I knew you'd want to know. I'm sure I'm the only one Mira told and she'll think I betrayed her confidence."

"Under the circumstances, Teresa, you've done the right thing. Every bit of information we acquire, the sooner we'll be able to find Destiny."

She wrote down Mira's phone number, address and where she worked. "I hope this helps. We're all so worried about Destiny."

Hawkman stuffed the paper into his pocket and rose. "Thank you, ladies. And if you hear anything else, please feel free to call me." He handed them two of his cards. "Would you like me to walk you to your car?"

They shook their heads. "No, that's fine," Grace said. "We're parked right in front."

Hawkman left the hall and headed for the Triple 'C'. He wanted to check if Ricardo had gone there after bingo. In less than twenty minutes, he walked in the door of the Indian casino, only to land in the midst of a brawl. Max had Tony Ricardo by the scruff of the neck and another guard held Roland Alexander in an arm lock. Struggling with the two yelling men, they hauled them toward the front door. Hawkman noticed that a couple of black and whites had pulled up at the entrance with their lights flashing. Each car held a pair of officers. They handcuffed the fighting men and one of the policemen held open the back door while the other loaded Ricardo into the first vehicle and Alexander into the second.

Max dusted off his hands as he marched back inside, followed by the guard and two officers. He glanced up with a surprised expression. "When did you get here? Didn't even see ya."

Hawkman chuckled. "Can't imagine why. Looks like you had your hands full. What was that all about?"

"I'll tell you shortly. Gotta go file a report." He pointed toward the side exit where they'd met once before. "Meet you outside in about ten minutes."

Hawkman went out the door and paced the sidewalk, wondering what had caused the fighting match between Roland Alexander and Tony Ricardo.

CHAPTER EIGHTEEN

Hawkman waited for almost thirty minutes before Max finally appeared.

"Sorry I took so long," he said, pulling a pack of cigarettes from his breast pocket and shaking his head. "Quite an ordeal."

"What happened?"

"No one really knows why the scuffle started. Ricardo and Alexander were seated at the same blackjack table. The dealer said they were angrily whispering back and forth, but she couldn't make out what they were saying because she had to concentrate on the whole table of customers. Even a couple of the patrons asked them to hold it down. Suddenly, she said, Alexander shoved Ricardo off his chair and told him to shut-up. By the time we got there, they were going at it with their fists."

"Did you hear anything that might indicate what they were fighting about?"

"I heard Ricardo spit out something to the effect that Alexander owed him money. Alexander told him he'd gotten plenty from his victims so to shut his damn mouth. They both got real quiet when our team of guards showed up."

"That's interesting. Wonder what he meant by victims?"

Max shrugged. "Could have meant anything from people he'd won from to who knows what. We could read anything into it."

"Yeah, you're right. How long had Alexander been here?"

"Most of the evening. Ricardo didn't arrive until shortly before the fight started."

Hawkman nodded. "That figures because Tony just left

the bingo hall a little while ago. I'm wondering if these two men are somehow involved in the disappearances of Destiny and Carmen." He told Max about the conversation he'd had with Teresa and Grace, also about his suspicions of why Ricardo made periodic trips up into the hills. He then told him about his visit to Dr. Crowley's office.

Max scratched his head. "I can see why the word 'victim' pushed your buttons. Especially when both those girls had money on them when they disappeared. So far, though, Carmen's check has never been cashed. However, what you just said gives me hope the girls might still be alive. Tony could be using those medications to keep them drugged. But where is he hiding them? And how does Alexander fit in?"

Hawkman hooked his thumbs in the front of his jeans' pockets. "Not sure how to answer either of your questions. But what really worries me is how long the girls will remain alive. We really need to hop on these clues fast. It's been a week tonight since Destiny disappeared."

Kicking a piece of gravel off the sidewalk, Max studied the ground for a few moments. "It's been longer for Carmen. If the women are being held up in the hills somewhere, it will take a long time to cover that area by foot or even in a vehicle. We either need a good bloodhound or I could try and get a helicopter."

Pushing his cowboy hat back, Hawkman squinted. "Start work on getting the helicopter. Talk to Tom Broadwell and tell him we're working together. Meanwhile, you just gave me a great idea. Can you get off Sunday?"

Max grinned. "You damned right I can. What time do you want to pick me up?"

"Say about noon. Bring your pistol. Got a hunting rifle with you?"

"No, only an assault weapon."

"Okay. I'll stick a couple in the truck."

"Sounds like old times, hunting for bigger game than animals." He glanced through the glass to the inside of the casino and sighed. "Guess I better get back to this hum-drum job so I don't get fired. Not quite ready for that yet."

Hawkman laughed and waved as he headed for the parking lot.

❧

Saturday morning, Hawkman called Mira Jones and found her home. He sensed she'd been warned that he might contact her as she didn't question him when he asked for an appointment. They agreed to meet at two o'clock at her residence.

He called Detective Williams to confirm that he had the subpoena for the medical files of Elsa and Marco Ricardo. Knowing the physician's office would be open until noon, they decided to meet there at ten, hoping to hasten the process.

Jennifer came into the room just as he hung up. He briefed her on what had happened and asked if she'd prepare sandwiches for Sunday, because they'd probably be gone the whole day.

"No problem," she said. "There's left-over roast beef from last night. I'll make them up and leave them in the refrigerator."

"That would be great. Sure you don't mind?"

"Not at all, on one condition."

He laughed. "I knew there'd be a catch." But when he looked at her, his voice sobered. "Why are you frowning?"

"Promise me you'll be extra careful and take your rifle as well your pistol. I don't like the idea of you going up into those hills. I've heard there are all kinds of riffraff guarding their marijuana fields, illegal labs and whatever else they can hide. And from what I hear, they shoot to kill."

Hawkman strolled over and put his arm around her shoulders. "You realize you're talking to an ex-agent who's seen worse than this. And I'll be accompanied by one of the best agents around. And on top of all that, I plan on taking my rifles, plus Rochester, Jesse's bloodhound."

She jerked up her head. "You're taking that dog? I bet he hasn't tracked in ages. Do you think he'll even remember how to work the field? You sure he won't be more of a hindrance than help?"

"That dog, as you call him, is a full-blooded hound in his prime. They never forget their mission in life. And when I smear his nose with Destiny's scent, there will be no stopping him."

"I hope you're not taking the new 4X4. And what does Max think about you bringing the dog?"

He grinned. "Boy, you're full of questions. He doesn't know it yet, but he'll love the idea. And no, I'm taking the old pick-up. It has 4-wheel drive and we'll look more like hunters riding in it. In fact, I'm driving it today so I can check it out and fill it up."

She rolled her eyes. "What if something happens to that animal? Rochester is like a member of their family."

"I'll talk to Jesse this afternoon. And nothing's going to happen. He knows if we don't get that hound off that front porch, he'll mourn himself to death. And who knows. That dog just might help us find Destiny."

Hawkman glanced at the wall clock. "I gotta go." He gave her a quick kiss, grabbed his hat off the shelf of the 'Hawkman Corner', shrugged into his leather jacket, and headed out the door. "Don't wait up."

Hawkman rolled up in front of Dr. Crowley's office and parked behind the detective's unmarked car. Williams opened the door and climbed out. "Where the hell you been?" he called.

Hawkman checked his watch as he jumped out of the truck. "It's only ten till ten. I'm early."

"Hell, I thought we decided to be here at nine thirty," he smirked.

Shaking his head, Hawkman chuckled. Williams had never been a good liar. "Well, then, I'm only twenty minutes late. How's traffic sound as a good excuse?"

"Pitiful in this part of the country," the detective said, grinning.

As the two men walked toward the entrance, Williams pulled the subpoena from his breast pocket. "We had Tony Ricardo and Roland Alexander brought in last night for disturbing the peace. No one pressed any charges, so we slapped them with a fine and released them."

"Yeah, I walked in the Triple 'C' just as the whole thing ended. But don't know what caused the scuffle. Max heard something about one owing the other money."

"They didn't say a word. Promised to pay the fine and left in a hurry."

The two men entered the waiting room and Elaine Chen's face turned ashen when she spotted Hawkman. It went through his mind that this girl definitely didn't like any type of police authority in her space or else his eye-patch made her nervous.

"May I help you?" she asked in a tense voice.

"Tell Dr. Crowley that Detective Williams wishes to see him." He flashed his badge as discreetly as possible.

Ms. Chen jumped up, almost knocking over her chair, and hurried down the hallway. She returned almost immediately. "Please follow me."

She led the two men to the office that Hawkman had visited before.

"Dr. Crowley will see you as soon as he finishes with his patient."

"Thank you," Williams said, his gaze following the girl as she closed the door. "That's one edgy young woman. Wonder why? You think maybe she has a record or there's something in her past she doesn't want the doctor or us to know about?"

Hawkman nodded. "Very possible. She acted the same way when I visited previously."

"Just out of curiosity, I might run a check on her when I get back to the station. Not that I'd cause her any problems, unless. . ." He shook his head and waved a hand in front of him. "Did you get her name?"

"Yeah, Elaine Chen."

Williams wrote it down and slipped the paper into his pocket just as the doctor entered the room.

Dr. Crowley's gaze immediately went to Hawkman. "Hello, Mr. Casey. I see you've returned with a detective." He gestured toward two chairs in front of the desk. "Won't you gentlemen please have a seat."

"I'm Detective Williams and am serving you with a subpoena to turn over the medical files of Elsa and Marco Ricardo." He handed the doctor the paper.

The man cleared his throat and glanced at the document. "I expected this. I hope you realize my father is in no condition to be charged with any sort of legal actions. I've gone through the Ricardos' files and found discrepancies during the same time my father was experiencing some drastic health problems."

Williams sat down and studied the doctor's face. "The case we're working on involves Tony, the son of the Ricardos. And at this point we're unable to tell you whether your father is directly involved or had any knowledge of what happened. Only as the case develops will we know anything. I imagine you have a lawyer."

The doctor stood with his arms folded. "Yes, I do."

The detective tapped his finger on the desk. "Then I'd leave it up to him to take whatever action might be needed."

The young Crowley drew in a deep breath and crossed over to the filing cabinet. He brought out two files and placed them in front of Williams. "I've made copies of everything."

Williams stood and handed Hawkman one of the bulky folders. "That's an excellent idea, Thank you for being so cooperative. And I'm very sorry to hear about your father's illness. He was well thought of in this community."

Dr. Crowley nodded, his expression solemn. "I hope to keep it that way."

They left the office and when Williams slid under the steering wheel of his car, Hawkman handed him the file. "I'll come by your office later today. I've got a few things to do beforehand. Maybe you'll have a chance to go through one of these before I get there. I'd suggest Marco's first."

Williams sighed. "And today was my day off."

Hawkman stepped back in mock surprise. "You're kidding? They actually gave you a day off?"

"Yeah. Big deal, huh?" He poked his head out the window. "Yet, they knew I had a subpoena to deliver. Clever bunch, right?"

"They've got your number," Hawkman said, chuckling. "In about twenty-four hours I might have some helpful information. I'll clue you in this afternoon."

The detective's eyes brightened. "Man, that's the best news I've heard. See ya later."

Hawkman checked his watch and realized they'd only been in the doctor's office about thirty minutes. He'd have time to run out and talk to Jesse before his meeting with Mira. He hopped in the truck and headed out of town.

When he arrived at the small farm, Rochester occupied his usual spot on the porch. Amanda sat on the ground below, drawing in the dirt with a stick. She didn't even look up as Hawkman approached. He could hear her soft voice singing a mournful song.

"Hello, Amanda. How are you today?"

"Hi, Mr. Hawk Man. I'm not very good. I miss my mommy. I think she's dead."

That comment squeezed his heart and he knelt down beside her. "What makes you say that?"

"My friends at school say my mommy is probably dead. She's been gone too long."

"Don't listen to those kids, you hear? We're searching and we're going to find your mother."

The little girl looked up at him, tears welling in her eyes. "I hope you don't find her dead."

Hawkman swallowed hard and stood. "Your grandpa around?"

She nodded. "He's in the house."

He went up the steps and Rochester didn't move. Reaching over, Hawkman rubbed the dog's head between his mournful eyes. "You gotta perk up boy. I'm gonna take you huntin' tomorrow."

The word 'huntin' must have meant something to the dog as he thumped his tail a couple of times on the plank porch.

Jesse limped out the door. "My God, I heard him thump his tail. That dog's alive. What'd you say to him?"

"Told him I was takin' him huntin'."

The old man raised a brow. "What'd you mean by that?"

Hawkman glanced down at Amanda. "Let's talk inside."

Jesse took the hard backed chair as Hawkman plopped down on the couch and slid the yearbook he'd borrowed onto the coffee table. "That little granddaughter of yours is hearing tales from her friends."

"Yeah, I know. I'm havin' trouble gettin' her off to school. She used to love it, but now she hates it. Last week she almost missed the bus three times."

"You know kids can be cruel. She'll probably get through it all right."

Jesse shook his head. "Not so sure. She's going more into herself every day. I worry about her. Just too young of a child to have this uncertainty about her mama."

"Keep her talking. That will help."

"I try, but she ignores me, goes outside and sits in the dirt drawing angel pictures. Told me yesterday that her mama's in heaven."

Hawkman cringed inwardly. "Amanda's just acting out her emotions. And that's healthy, because she's at least getting them out. If she held them inside, then you might have more of a problem."

"She keeps telling me her mama's dead. And I don't know how to respond. I can't lie to the child. So what does one say?"

"I don't know what to tell you, Jesse." Hawkman lifted his hat, ran a hand over his head, then plopped it back on. "We're not much closer to finding Destiny, but I've heard some positive things. Can't tell you what they are right now. But I'm checking out every lead I get." He sighed. "This has been a rough case."

The old man nodded. "I hear rumors that you've got Tony Ricardo under investigation."

"Yes, you're right. It's made me mighty suspicious after

finding that picture of him and Destiny. By the way, thanks for lending me the photo and yearbook. I've made copies, so I won't need them anymore. But that's not what I want to talk to you about. I want to borrow Rochester tomorrow."

Jesse raised his brows. "You serious about taking that dog huntin'?"

"Very much so. Want to take him up in the hills."

The old man's face clouded. "You think my Destiny's buried up there?"

"No, quite the contrary. I suspect she might be held captive somewhere. But we've got to find her before something does happen. Has that dog lost his tracking abilities?"

Jesse smacked his leg with his palm. "Not in the slightest. He's gotten better with age. Men around here take him out all the time and can't get over what a good trackin' hound he is."

"That's good news. What I need is something with Destiny's scent on it. Preferably clothes that haven't been washed. Is that a possibility?"

"Yep," the old man said, struggling to stand with the aid of his cane. "Haven't touched a thing in her room. So she's bound to have a few clothes in her hamper."

Hawkman motioned for him to sit back down. "Don't worry about it now. Put the garments in a plastic bag and I'll pick them up along with Rochester tomorrow morning about ten o'clock. Can you supply me with a small bag of dog food to last the whole day? I'll bring the water."

Jesse stared at Hawkman. "You've got something up your sleeve. I see it in your face."

He nodded. "Yes. But, I'm not going to get your hopes up, because I could be barking up the wrong tree."

The pun made Jesse grin. "I'll have everything ready."

Hawkman left the farm house with the old man's blessings. Now, he'd head for Mira Jones' place.

CHAPTER NINETEEN

Hawkman arrived in front of Mira Jones' apartment at a quarter to two. He made his way through the front archway and surveyed the area. The two story buildings arranged in a circle appeared old, but well maintained and recently painted. They surrounded a yard that sported manicured shrubs and newly cut grass. A play area in the center of the lawn included a swing, slide and jungle gym placed on a soft layer of wood chips.

It appeared there were four apartments in each building: two above and two below. The structures were well-spaced from each other which would help the noise factor. He knew this type of housing was hard to come by and suspected they were on the high end of the rent scale. Nice place, he thought.

Hawkman found 12A on the first floor of the second stack of apartments and knocked. He stood back and waited. Shortly, a pretty, bright-eyed young black woman opened the door and greeted him with a big smile.

"Hi, Mr. Casey. I recognize you from bingo. I was there the night you came with Jennifer. We all wondered what her private investigator husband looked like. You didn't disappoint us." She grinned, stepped aside and waved him forward. "Come on in."

The aroma of something delicious hit him in the face. "What are you cooking? It smells wonderful."

She laughed. "Just pulled an apple pie from the oven. Would you like a piece?"

"I know this sounds presumptuous, but, yes."

Pointing to the couch, she headed for a door leading off the dining room. "Make yourself comfortable, I'll be right back."

Within a few moments she returned carrying two plates

loaded with steaming apple pie, topped with ice cream. "Here you go," she said, placing a helping in front of him on the coffee table. "Let me get us a cup of coffee to go with that. Cream and sugar?"

"No, thanks. Black is fine," Hawkman said, eager to dive into the delicacy.

Mira brought in two mugs of the steaming brew. "Now, enjoy and then we'll talk."

Hawkman glanced at her between bites. "I know why you were named after a star, this is absolutely wonderful." He noted a blush on Mira's dark skin.

"Thank you. Glad you like it."

Hawkman took a small recorder from his pocket and placed it on the table. "I'm sure you know why I'm here. Hope you don't mind if I record our conversation. I hate trying to decipher my notes."

"No, I don't mind. I'm sure it's much easier to remember that way. And, yes, Teresa called and said you might want to know what Tony said to me that night at the Triple 'C'." She wiped her lips with a napkin. "I know I should have come to you first with the information, because it's been worrying me ever since."

"What did Tony say to you exactly?"

She put a finger in the air and cocked her head. "First of all, he was drunk. But he said he didn't know why all the fuss over Destiny. The woman was alive and well." Mira shook her head and closed her eyes. "I could hardly believe those words came out of his mouth. I asked him how he could say that when no one had seen Destiny for a week. He told me to believe it. He knew it for a fact."

"Did he say anything that might indicate where he'd gotten that information?"

Mira shook her head. "No, he didn't say another word. Finished playing that slot machine, slapped it with his hand and staggered away. He did stop down the aisle aways and talked to Ginny. Then I didn't see him again."

"Who's Ginny? Does she play bingo too?"

"Yes, she always sits right in front of the caller. She's a white girl with straight dark brown hair that hangs just below her collar. I don't know her last name, but she usually puts the numbers up on the board for the hot ball."

Hawkman nodded. "Yes, I remember now. You have any idea what he said to her?"

"No, but I could tell she brushed him off, because he walked away rather briskly. Ginny can't stand him."

Hawkman ate the last bite off his plate and set the dish down. "Have you heard from others who spoke to Tony?"

"No. People are a bit leery and avoid him since he's been associated with Destiny's disappearance."

"How'd you find out we had him under suspicion?"

She grinned. "I heard Rene talking about it."

Hawkman stood. "Mira, I want to thank you for this very important information. I pray Tony does know what he's talking about. The thing that worries me is how he can be so sure she's alive."

She walked him to the door. "Oh, by the way, in case you're interested, Manette Riley is the lady who took care of Tony's parents the last few weeks they were alive."

This bit of information piqued his interest. "Who's Manette Riley?"

Mira laughed. "Do you recall the lady who yelled bingo in a very unique fashion the night you were there?" She rolled her eyes. "Everyone knows when Manette gets a bingo."

He chuckled. "Oh yeah. I almost jumped out of my chair. Does she live around here?"

"Yes. Let me get her address for you." Mira headed back toward the kitchen near the phone where she flipped open a book and jotted down the details. She crossed back to Hawkman and handed him the slip of paper. "I added her phone number, in case she's not home. Would you like me to call and see if she's there right now?"

"I'd appreciate it. I'll wait outside."

"Okay, give me a second."

Within a few moments Mira came to the door. "She's home and will be expecting you."

Hawkman checked the address and pointed up the street. "Her place is just a couple of blocks over, isn't it?"

Mira nodded. "That's right."

Hawkman handed her a business card. "If you hear anything that involves Destiny or this case, I'd appreciate a call. You can reach me here. If I'm not in the office, the message is routed to my home. So, call any time." He touched his hat. "And thank you for that delicious piece of apple pie. I thoroughly enjoyed it."

"You're more than welcome. We're all praying for Destiny's safe return. And I promise the next time I hear anything, I'll come straight to you."

Hawkman waved as he strolled toward his truck. He then drove to Manette's house which reminded him of a small cottage in a fairy tale book. It sat back off the street and the narrow sidewalk to the front door wound its way through an archway of climbing roses. Two white outdoor plastic chairs rested on the concrete porch and a large calico cat lounged on the wide ledge of one of the windows. When Hawkman stepped up to the door, the cat yawned, stretched his paws forward, then leaped from his perch and stood at Hawkman's feet as if he were the visitor. The minute the door opened, the feline bounded inside.

"Cally, you get yourself back outside right this minute," the woman yelled. "Oh, come in, Mr. Casey. I've got to catch that little varmint." She opened the door and left him alone as she scurried after the animal.

Hawkman could hear her musical laughter coming from different parts of the house as she chased the cat from room to room. He stood in the foyer until she finally returned carrying the feline. Out of breath, she shook her head and put Cally outside.

"That cat is spoiled rotten." She closed the door and glanced up at him grinning. "Sorry about that. But if I don't make her go out for a few hours during the day, she'd never get any fresh air or sunshine. She's without doubt an indoor cat."

"No problem," Hawkman said, chuckling.

She gestured toward the living room. "Have a seat and I'll get us a cup of coffee."

Manette had a slim figure and a beautiful face covered with flawless bronze skin and few wrinkles. He judged her to be around fifty, but hard to tell with those mischievous eyes that twinkled with delight. Her contagious smile had him grinning without effort.

Hawkman ambled toward an overstuffed chair opposite the couch and sat down. He glanced around the small neat room, and noted the furniture had that 'lived-in' look. He liked it and immediately felt comfortable. The shelves on one wall were crammed with what he assumed to be family pictures. A bouquet of real flowers sat on the small oblong oak coffee table. Manette soon joined him, carrying two steaming mugs.

"Milk or sugar?" she asked.

"No, black is fine."

She set the cups on the table and took a seat on the couch opposite him. "Mira said you're interested in Tony Ricardo's parents."

Hawkman put the recorder on the coffee table. "Hope you don't mind if I record our conversation, I'm a terrible note taker."

"Don't mind at all."

"I'm not particularly interested in his parents, but more about where you took care of them. Did you go to their house in the country?"

She shook her head. "No, Tony hired me after he moved his folks into town. He'd rented them a nice two bedroom apartment. At first, he had me check on them once a day. But as the poor things grew weaker, he wanted me there all day to cook their meals and take care of their personal needs."

Hawkman sipped on the hot brew. "So you couldn't tell me where they lived before they moved into the apartment?"

Setting her cup on the table, Manette pushed some strands of loose black hair underneath the bright colored band she wore around her head. "I did go out to the country place one time with old man Ricardo. He could still drive when they first got into town. The missus was the sickest at that time and he couldn't take care of her alone. Anyway, he wanted to go to the place in the country, as he called it, and get some stuff. I don't even remember now what he needed. But he wanted me to go and help load it. So I said I would."

"Do you remember how you got to the house?"

She smacked her hands down on her thighs. "You know, I didn't drive on that trip, so didn't pay much attention. But I know we took the freeway south, then took an exit that headed off onto some dirt road that went up into the hills." She waved her hand. "Rougher than a cob and isolated to beat hell. I thought we'd never get there."

"So you rode quite aways on a rough country road?"

"It seemed like it. But I remember we did turn up another winding road and I recall thinking at that time, I'd never be able to find my way out of this place if something happened to the old man while we were there." She let out one of her laughs. "However, we returned safe and sound."

"What did the house look like?"

She looked up at the ceiling, gnawing her lower lip. "You couldn't see the cabin from the road as it sat back so far and was surrounded by huge trees. It just blended into the mountain side." She tapped her cheek with her forefinger. "I shouldn't call it a cabin, because it was bigger than that." She spread her arms apart and gestured with her hands. "It had a huge living room and kitchen. And I know we gathered stuff out of three bedrooms. There were probably more rooms, but we didn't go into any of the others."

"Was the place furnished?"

"Oh yeah. I think all they moved out of there were their clothes and personal stuff. Tony furnished the apartment in town before he brought them down. He said that maybe one day he'd move up to the big house."

"Where did Tony get the money to rent an apartment and pay for your services?"

She shrugged. "I have no idea, but he paid me by the week

in cash and always on time. I have my suspicions that his folks were pretty wealthy."

"How do you know that?"

Furrowing her brow, she stared into his face. "You know, now that you ask, I guess I just assumed it. I don't know what the older Ricardos did during their lifetime. It just appeared they had money. Tony did a lot of gambling and had to get the bucks from somewhere." She threw her hands in the air. "He sure doesn't hold a job that anybody knows about, so everyone just figured it had to be his folks."

Hawkman nodded. "I can see where people would come up with that conclusion." He finished his cup of coffee and placed the mug carefully on the small table. "As the Ricardos' illnesses progressed, did you end up spending twenty-four hours a day with them?"

"No, Tony stayed there at night."

"Did you take care of the older Ricardos until they died?"

She shook her head. "I had some personal problems at that time and had to quit about a week before they passed away. Such a shame. I think they actually committed suicide."

"That bad, huh?"

"They were in a lot of pain near the end."

"Didn't the doctor prescribe pain killers and sleeping pills?"

"Oh, yes. They had plenty of potent medications. But they'd both told me that this wasn't living. They felt they'd suffered enough. In fact, Tony only left twelve hours worth of pills with me each day. I don't know what he did with the rest. But he warned me they might take more when I wasn't looking. And, from the autopsy report, it looks like that's what happened 'cause they overdosed." She shook her head sadly. "That's why I feel in my heart they'd made a suicide pact."

"How do you think they got their hands on enough pills to do that?"

She lifted her hands in question. "Oh, probably at night when Tony went to sleep, they'd steal a few out of the bottle and stash them somewhere. Saved them up until they had enough to do the job. Believe me, they were alert right up until the time I left. They were just in horrible pain."

Hawkman stood and picked up the the recorder. "Manette, I really appreciate you seeing me at such short notice. You've given me valuable information."

She frowned. "I hope it helps find Destiny. Do you think she's still alive?"

He raised his hand with fingers crossed. "We never give up. Thanks for the coffee."

Manette saw him to the door and when Cally ran back inside, she threw her arms in the air. "I give up. The damn cat is in for the night."

Hawkman laughed as he headed toward his truck.

When he reached the police station, he found Williams sitting at his desk absorbed in one of the files they'd taken from the doctor's office.

"Find anything interesting?" Hawkman said, pulling up a chair.

"Hell, yes. Old Dr. Crowley prescribed heavy pain and sleep medications to Elsa and Marco Ricardo right up until four months ago."

"That's around the time that young Crowley took over," Hawkman said.

"We can't go after the old man as that would be a civil case and the police don't do those. He obviously didn't know what he was doing and the only one who might be interested in pursuing that action would be Tony. But, I doubt he'd be interested if he had an ulterior motive."

"I agree. I spoke with the pharmacist who dispensed the medications and he said Tony always picked up the prescriptions. So, I think it's time we question Ricardo." Hawkman paused. "However, I'd like you to wait until Monday."

The detective raised a brow. "Why's that?"

Hawkman told him about his plan with Max Pritchard and about the conversations he'd had with Mira Jones and Manette Riley. "If we see Tony or find what he's hiding in those hills, I'd like to take him by surprise."

"You gotta point. I don't know how much ground you can cover up in that rough terrain. A dog will obviously help. But what you need is a helicopter."

"Yeah, I've got that in mind."

The detective scowled. "I hope you don't think our department can furnish one. Those things cost a fortune to operate. And so far, this case doesn't warrant that type of spending. I can possibly spare some men if you find something."

Hawkman looked at him with fake surprise. "You mean you don't have aircraft stored in a hanger just waiting to be used?"

Williams laughed. "Yeah, right."

"Max and I talked about procuring a chopper through the Agency, that is, if we don't have any luck tomorrow. So you're off the hook."

"Whew, that's a relief," William said, wiping his brow. Then he raised his hand. "Oh, I almost forgot, I ran a check on Elaine Chen."

"Find anything?"

"Chen has worked at that office for close to five years. She could be well aware that old doc Crowley wrote prescriptions for dead people. If she knew and didn't report it, that might give her plenty of reasons for worry."

Hawkman nodded. "That could concern her. In fact, I'd bet my last dollar on it. She's got a stable job and I'm sure she'd hate to lose it. So each time some sort of law enforcement or authority enters that office, her nerves go on edge."

"Unfortunately for her, the way this case is going, she'll need to be questioned. If this comes down to a murder trial with Tony involved, she'll more than likely end up testifying in court."

"Yep. A hard lesson to learn if you've withheld vital information."

"Also, I thought it interesting that she drives a new car, and purchased a home a year ago. Her parents live there, along with her young child, but no record of a husband. So how can she afford all these luxuries on her salary?"

Hawkman leaned forward, resting his arms on the desk. "Maybe the parents have money. I heard many of these immigrants come over here loaded with cash."

Williams sighed. "Yeah, that's a possibility."

Hawkman pointed at the Ricardo's file. "Anything in those I should look at?"

The detective shrugged. "The old doc did record giving the Ricardos prescriptions. Who knows what he might have omitted. But it looks like young Ricardo has enough drugs to last six months or more."

Hawkman rubbed his chin. "There were several bottles in his medicine cabinet. I wonder where he stores the rest."

Williams leaned back in his chair. "I'm not going to ask how you know that. But I have the feeling that you're thinking that if he's the one who kidnapped the women, he's keeping them drugged. Can you tell me what the hell for?"

"The information that I've come upon makes me think he's involved in some sort of kinky sexual games. What worries me is when he tires of this group, what does he do next? Kill them and bury them in the hills?"

Williams shook his head and sighed. "Do you think he's working alone?"

"No. In fact, from what I've learned about him, I doubt he could mastermind something so complicated. I've got my eye on several others."

The detective came to attention. "Who?"

"I'll let you know when I have more evidence."

Williams slumped back in his chair. "I hate it when you do that."

Hawkman chuckled. "I don't want you harassing anyone who might not be involved with this mess." He rose, leaning his hands on the desk. "I'll have my cell phone with me tomorrow. Not sure how good it will operate in the hills, but if I need your help, I'll try to get through somehow."

"I'll be waiting."

Hawkman headed home and when he got to Ager Beswick road leading into Copco Lake, he slowed and stayed alert for any deer that might jump out of the darkness. Suddenly, a loud blast sounded and the window on the passenger side of the truck shattered.

CHAPTER TWENTY

"What the hell!" he shouted, automatically ducking as he pulled his ,45 from his shoulder holster.

Hawkman felt another shot hit the bed of the truck. Steering in a zig zag pattern, he hoped to give the impression he'd been hit. He rounded a bend and veered as close to the mountainside as possible and still remain on the shoulder. Shutting off the headlights, he killed the engine, and jumped out.

He knew the bullets had come from his right, so he hunkered down on the left side of the truck. Hearing no more rounds being fired, he made a dash toward the opposite side of the road, then leaped down the steep embankment, using the scrub oaks as hand holds to keep from tumbling into the lake. His sight soon adjusted to the darkness and he cautiously made his way back to where he figured the first shot had originated.

About two hundred yards ahead, he spotted some headlights flickering through the trees where he remembered a partial road had been cut into the rocky mountainside by a hopeful builder. Only a four-wheel drive could make it up that primitive path. If he didn't hurry, they'd be gone before he'd have a chance to catch a glimpse of the vehicle. Even though leery about exposing himself on the roadway at this time of night holding his pistol, he decided to chance it and climbed up to the asphalt. He'd just put a foot on the edge of the shoulder when he spotted headlight beams up ahead. They cut into the darkness like a knife as the vehicle rounded a curve coming toward Copco Lake.

"Damn," he muttered, and slid back into the shadows. He

struggled along the incline, making little progress, but kept an eye on the lights he could still see through the trees on the hillside. It appeared they were having a problem coming down; either too little room to turn around, or possibly had hit high center on a rock. All of which benefited him.

Once the oncoming car passed, Hawkman jumped upon the road and ran toward the lights now advancing rapidly down the hill. He could see he'd never make it in time to get a good look at the license plate before it moved onto the main road. Not sure they were the ones who'd shot at his truck, he didn't dare risk firing a warning.

Hawkman spotted another approaching car in the distance. He continued running, but moved over to the shoulder so he could duck into the trees at any moment. All he could hope for was that the oncoming car would round the bend about the same time the 4X4 hit the road. Then he would at least be able to tell the make and color of the vehicle, even if he couldn't read the plates.

As the oncoming lights got closer, he dropped over the shoulder into the shadows. Almost losing his footing on the soft dirt of the steep incline, he grabbed the trunk of a small tree to keep from rolling down the grade. He righted himself just in time to see the 4X4 pass in front of the car and turn toward town. He immediately recognized it as a late model, light colored Toyota 4-Runner. Now where the hell had he seen it?

Hawkman stayed hidden and watched the Toyota until it rounded the bend and disappeared from his sight. He waited for the other car to pass before jumping onto the road and trotting back to his truck. No sense in trying to catch the 4-runner. It had too big of a lead, so he headed toward the lake. He swore he'd seen that vehicle before, but where? For the life of him, he couldn't jog his memory.

When he walked in the door, he found Jennifer pacing the living room in her gown and robe. She glanced at him with relief. "Thank goodness, you're here. I heard some shots echoing across the lake about thirty minutes ago. It worried me because you weren't home yet."

He hung up his hat and ran a hand through this hair. "Yeah, someone fired a few potshots."

She frowned and put her hands on her hips. "At you?"

He nodded, shrugging out of his jacket. "Shattered the glass on the truck's passenger side window and I have a couple of dents in the truck bed.

"This case is getting more dangerous by the day. I don't like it one bit."

"You're right. And I don't want you to let your guard down. I'm getting too close and they're getting nervous."

"Do you have any idea who's behind it?"

"I have my suspicions, but I'm not saying."

"Oh, you make me so angry when you do that."

He grinned. "You sound like Williams. Come on, let's go to bed. I have a full day tomorrow."

❧

The next morning, Hawkman dressed in his hunting camouflage, secured two rifles on the rack across the back window of the old pick-up and stored extra ammunition behind the seat. He grabbed the sandwiches Jennifer had made from the refrigerator along with a couple of soft drinks, then filled three canteens with water.

Arriving at Jesse's place at ten, he noticed the old man appeared tired as he thumped through the house with his cane. He grumbled something about Amanda as he came into the living room carrying a plastic bag.

"Didn't hear you, Jesse. What'd you say about Amanda?"

"I had a time with her this morning."

"Where is she?"

"The neighbor lady down the road is worried about her as much as I am. She and her little girl wanted Amanda to go shopping with them, hopin' that might perk her up. But she didn't want to go and sulked around here until I scolded her to get dressed."

Hawkman took a deep breath. "She's going to be all right, Jesse. Just give her some time."

"I hope you're right." He sighed and held out the bag. "Here's the clothes I found in Destiny's hamper." Then he pointed with his cane at a paper sack by the door. "There's the food for Rochester. Hope we can get that dog off the porch and into your truck."

"Hawkman glanced toward the front door. "Fortunately, a bloodhound's instinct to hunt and track is mighty strong." Then he looked back at Jesse. "Don't you use a whistle with him?"

The old fellow snapped his fingers. "I almost forgot. Of course, that will do it. It's been a long time since I've been huntin'. Hold on a second." He limped into the kitchen and came back with a police whistle attached to a long leather thong, wiped it down his overalls and handed it to him. "Got a little dusty just hangin' there not gettin' any use."

"No problem," Hawkman said.

"Give it three short blasts when you want Rochester to come. But just wave your hand to have him move into the field." Jesse displayed a pushing motion, palm out. "You want things quiet when he starts. Here's a long leash in case he doesn't want to mind. Sometimes these hounds get stubborn."

Hawkman pulled the leather strap over his head, letting the whistle rest on his chest. He rolled up the tether and tucked it into his hunting coat pocket. "We'll know in a few minutes if it will work." Carrying the bag of Destiny's clothes, he picked up the sack of dog food and headed out the door. He placed the items in the jump seat of the truck, then went around and dropped the tailgate so the dog could jump in.

Jesse watched from the door as Hawkman blasted the whistle three times. Rochester's ears perked and he raised his snout off his paws.

"Come on boy," Hawkman said, slapping his thighs. "Let's go hunting."

The dog's tail thumped on the wooden planks and he slowly rose off his haunches.

"Come on," Hawkman coached. "Let's go."

Rochester let out a howl and loped down the steps. Leaping

into the back of the truck without hesitation, he settled down on an old rug that Hawkman had placed there earlier.

Closing the tailgate, Hawkman gave Jesse the thumbs up sign.

He waved and turned back into the house. Hawkman knew the old man would spend the rest of the day praying for his daughter.

At eleven thirty, Hawkman pulled into one of the vacant parking slots in front of Prichard's apartment. Even though he'd arrived a few minutes early, he figured Max would be eagerly waiting. He had that pegged right. Before he could raise his fist to knock, the door opened and a smiling face greeted him.

"I thought the time would never roll around. What took you so long?"

Hawkman laughed. "Had to go pick up the bloodhound."

Max's eyes lit up like neon signs as he glanced toward the truck. "You're kidding!"

"Nope. Old Rochester is napping in the pick-up bed, preparing himself for a long hunting trip."

He cuffed Hawkman on the shoulder. "Oh, man, this is going to be great. Let me get my jacket."

Slipping on the camouflage hunting coat, Max buttoned it to conceal his shoulder holster. "You got the rifles?"

"Oh, yeah. Jennifer wouldn't let me out of the house without them."

"You gotta great gal," he said winking. "When do I get to meet her?"

"As soon as we solve this case, I'll have you out for dinner. But just remember, she's taken."

When Max walked around the rear of the truck, he glanced at the bloodhound snuggled down on a rug. He smiled, then opened the door to the passenger side and eyed the shattered window. "This happen recently?" he asked, closing the door carefully.

"Yeah, last night. Got shot at on the road going home."

"Hmm, sounds like you're getting too close for comfort."

"I sure as hell hope so." Hawkman said, handing Max a

map he'd tucked between the seat and console. "Detective Williams had this blueprint of the area I'd like to scout. It's thickly wooded. The police have made several raids looking for drugs and labs. The marijuana fields are heavily guarded and the guys shoot to kill. Take a look at it."

Max glanced at him before taking the folded paper. "Sounds like pretty mean territory."

"Yeah, so we want to stay alert every minute. To cover our butts, I had the detective give us permission slips to hunt in the 'no hunting' posted areas. Don't know if it'll stand up in court, but we'll take our chances."

"You always were the brains of a mission. I'd have never thought of that."

"I want us to appear as a pair of hunters."

Max pointed toward the rear. "Hey, we've even got the dog."

Hawkman nodded. "You think of anything we've forgotten?"

"How about we grab some sandwiches at a fast food place."

Pointing behind the seat at a brown paper bag, Hawkman grinned. "All taken care of, along with water, sodas and food for the dog."

"Sounds like you've got everything under control."

"Well, shall we hit the road?"

While traveling down Interstate 5, Hawkman showed Max the hand-drawn map he'd found in Ricardo's truck. "I want you to store this sketch in your memory before we get to the exit. It's hard to make out, but I think it means something. Just got to figure out the directions. I'm hoping once we've canvassed the area, maybe it'll make sense."

Max examined the paper, turning it around several times. "You're right, can't make heads or tails out of all the lines. I'll keep it in mind as we move along."

Hawkman pointed toward the dashboard. "Stick it in the glove compartment. We might want to check it later."

Max then took a pair of binoculars from his pocket and pulled the strap over his head so the glasses rested on his chest.

Within the hour, they turned off the highway where Hawkman had seen Ricardo leave the freeway, and head toward the hills. The pavement soon gave way to a dirt and gravel road. He thought about Manette's description of driving to the Ricardo's place. It fit the pattern.

The men scrutinized each house as they passed. Most looked deserted, but when one appeared occupied, they stopped and asked questions. The people were cautious. They denied seeing a dark green Dodge pickup pass their place or anything suspicious going on in their area.

Leaving the homes behind, Hawkman continued driving up the bumpy trail. He kept his eye peeled for any side road that shot off into the hills. He'd seen several and planned to explore them soon. Max kept the binoculars to his eyes scanning the area when suddenly he pointed ahead.

"Somebody's been up here recently. That imprint in the grass was made not long ago by a good sized vehicle. It wouldn't stay flat that way for much over a couple of days."

Hawkman nodded. "I see it. Someone could have come up here bird hunting or it could very well have been Tony in his truck."

Max grabbed his binoculars as they bounced hard off his breast bone. "This is some rough territory. We're not going to be able to cover much of it before sundown."

The trail narrowed to a rough path. Hawkman pulled over to the side and stopped. "I think we'll go on foot now."

He jumped out and released the dog from the back letting him run for a few minutes while he and Max lifted the rifles from the rack across the back window. Leaning his gun against the fender, Hawkman gave the dog a small bit of dried food, then poured water into a metal container he'd thrown in for this purpose. When the dog finished, Hawkman reached into the jump seat of the truck and removed the plastic bag containing Destiny's garments. He opened it and called Rochester. Squatting down, he passed the clothes in front of the dog's nose.

The hound bayed, then immediately dropped his snout to the ground. Hawkman gave the silent hand signal and the animal headed for the trees. Tucking Destiny's things back into the plastic bag, he stuck it into the game pouch of his jacket. He and Max grabbed their rifles, held them across their chests, and trotted after the bloodhound.

CHAPTER TWENTY-ONE

The two men had lost sight of the hound and were uncertain which way to head. They proceeded cautiously, keeping their eyes peeled for any sign of movement. Suddenly, from the side, a small two point buck crashed through the brush, making Max and Hawkman jerk around and aim their rifles. The deer, as startled as the men, leaped over a fallen log and disappeared into the wilderness.

Max glanced at Hawkman. "Wonder what frightened him right into our path?"

"Something startled that buck more than our scent. Wonder if Rochester scared him?"

Max headed in the direction from which the animal had burst through the foliage. "Let's check it out."

They'd tramped several hundred feet when Hawkman grabbed Max's arm. "Stop."

"Why?"

"Listen. You hear that?"

Max cocked his head. "Yeah, sounds like moaning."

"That's Rochester. Damn, I hope he isn't hurt." Hawkman stood silently, turning his head from side to side, concentrating on which direction the sound came as it bounced off the surrounding hills. Within a few seconds, he pointed to his left. "Let's try this way."

They hurriedly pushed through the thick foliage and soon came to a small meadow where the sound of the dog's baying became more pronounced. Stepping to the edge of the opening, but still hidden by the overhanging trees, Hawkman put a finger to his lips and dropped to his haunches. He took a small pair of binoculars from his pocket and studied the region.

He pointed straight ahead. "That area is posted with 'no hunting' signs all around the base of that hill. And there's Rochester right in the middle of it, prancing around a pile of tree branches, howling like crazy."

"Yeah, I see him," Max said, taking his glasses away from his eyes. "Wonder what type of game is hidden in there to get him so excited?"

"I don't know, but he's supposed to be tracking Destiny's scent and that bothers me. I think we better go take a look. We'll skirt around the border of the clearing and stay out of sight." His expression grim, Hawkman flipped off the safety of his rifle and led the way.

Senses alert and using the shadows as their cover, the two men moved cautiously toward the hound. Suddenly, Hawkman jumped behind a large oak tree, put the dog whistle to his lips and blew three shrill blasts.

"What the hell?" Max said, as he stepped next to Hawkman.

He pointed up and to the left of Rochester. "I just caught the glint of a gun barrel moving along that ridge. I don't want anything happening to that hound. More than likely someone heard his yelping and has come to investigate."

The dog turned his head toward their direction and Hawkman blew the whistle again. Rochester lifted his snout and bayed a couple more times before he finally gave up on his siege and bounded toward the trees.

"So what's the next step?" Max asked.

"I'm hoping they'll see him head back this way and figure the hunters have given up."

The hound, with his snout to the ground, found his way to the two men hidden deep in the shadows.

"Good boy," Hawkman said, patting the animal's head. He then hooked the leash to the dog's collar and led him deeper into the shadows. Rochester followed obediently, shaking his head and throwing slobber from both sides of his jowls.

Hawkman secured the tether to a tree trunk, giving the canine enough leeway to roam only a few feet. He and Max then made their way back to the edge of the clearing and hid behind a large boulder. They focused their binoculars on the brush pile that Rochester wanted to attack. Hawkman poked Max and pointed toward a man dressed in camouflage walking from behind the stacked trees. An assault rifle hung from a strap over his shoulder and he carried a long stick that he kept jabbing around the edges of the barrier. Soon, a covey of quail flew upward, clicking their warning signal. Then his attention went to a net cover that had been thrown over the branches. He worked for several minutes tucking it tightly around the bottom.

Once he'd completed that job, he put the binoculars hanging around his neck to his eyes. He slowly turned in the direction of Hawkman and Max. The two men quickly ducked their heads behind the rock. Giving the sentry a couple of minutes, Hawkman peeked around the side and gave Max the go ahead sign. They eased up and watched the man ascend the hill. He soon disappeared in the dense growth.

"There's no telling how long Rochester howled before we heard him. Why the hell didn't that guy shoot him?" Max asked.

"He more than likely figured the dog belonged to a hunter and he didn't want to bring attention to whatever's hidden in that pile. Then, when he heard the whistle, he figured the hound would leave." Hawkman glanced at his watch, then looked up at the overcast sky. "It's going to be dark sooner than usual with this cloud cover. I better bring Rochester with us. Don't want some mountain lion making a meal out of Jesse's dog. He'd never forgive me."

Max nodded. "Good idea."

Rochester had wound around the tree to the point where he only had about two feet of rope left. The dog sat on his hindquarters, his mouth open with strands of drool dripping off the tip of his tongue.

Hawkman handed Max his rifle, untied the leash from the

tree, but left the tether hooked to the hound's collar. He folded the long cord in a figure eight and looped it around his belt, leaving enough slack so that he could keep the animal reined in close to his side. Taking a canteen of water from his game pouch, he took a swig, then poured some into his hand for the dog.

Once Hawkman had everything situated, he retrieved his gun from Max and the threesome started their journey back to the mysterious heap of branches. They hiked within the trees until they were almost there, then Hawkman again scanned the hillside with his binoculars. When he saw no sign of life, he motioned for Max to head toward the back side of the brush pile. Rochester lifted his head as if to howl and Hawkman quickly quieted him by clamping his mouth shut with his hand. "Quiet, boy," he whispered. "Can't have you giving us away."

They worked their way around, staying hidden as much as possible. Soon they were standing behind a full thatch of tree limbs. Rochester whimpered, dropped down on his belly and inched forward. Almost yanking the leash from Hawkman's hand, the dog abruptly lurched through a small opening of branches. Hanging on to his rifle, Hawkman dropped to his knees and looked inside.

"Oh my God!"

Max knelt beside him. "What is it?"

Hawkman yanked off the camouflage netting then tugged on branches that appeared to be woven together. "Help me pull these away. Looks like Destiny's car is under this mess."

"Let's pray she's not inside," Max said, standing his rifle next to Hawkman's.

Within a few minutes, they uncovered two small cars hidden in the underbrush. Max face turned ashen. "This other vehicle is Carmen's."

The two men worked frantically clearing off the rest of the limbs so they could get to the car doors. Just about the time they reached the passenger side of Destiny's Escort, Rochester let out a low growl deep in his throat, his back hairs bristling.

Hawkman whirled around and found himself face to face with the barrel of an assault rifle.

CHAPTER TWENTY-TWO

"Put hands above head," the man demanded in broken English. "What you doing here? This property private."

Hawkman and Max raised their arms and walked slowly toward him. "Why are you hiding these cars?" Hawkman asked.

"Not hiding. Protecting from sun and rain."

"That's a lie," Max said, dropping his arms and pointing at the vehicles. "They belong to two missing women. You're concealing police evidence."

"Keep hands up," The man said, poking Max in the chest with the barrel of his gun. "What you mean, conceal evidence? You police?"

"No," Max retorted. "But, you're in deep trouble."

At that moment, Hawkman felt the leash he'd twisted around his belt slip away and out of the corner of his eye spotted the hound scooting under Destiny's Escort. He took a chance, not knowing if the dog even understood the command and yelled, "Sic 'em, Rochester!"

The man jerked around as the dog lunged out from under the car baring his teeth. That was all the time Hawkman needed. He knocked the assault rifle upwards and threw a fist into the man's stomach that sent him to his knees.

Max grabbed the gun, pushed the guy face down, and placed a booted foot on his neck. "Don't move," he ordered, pointing the barrel at the man's head.

"I no move. Please, no kill me."

"What else are you protecting around here?"

"Only cars."

"How many guards are there?"

"Just me."

Max shoved his boot deeper into the man's neck. "That's hard to believe. You can't stand watch for twenty-four hours straight, you need rest."

"I sleep at night. Only patrol during day when hunters out."

Hawkman unhooked the leash from Rochester's collar and used the cord to tie the man's wrists and ankles. He and Max dragged their prisoner to a nearby tree and secured him to the trunk.

Walking around in the open area, Hawkman tried to get a dial tone on his cell phone, but to no avail. It meant they'd have to drive into town with their prisoner and turn him over to Williams, then lead the authorities back to get the cars.

Hawkman shook his head in frustration. "Damn, too many hills. Can't get anything but static."

Max let out an audible sigh and rubbed a hand across his chin. "Before we head back with this guy, we've got to search the inside of these cars. Gotta make sure the girls aren't there."

Hawkman nodded. "Fortunately, there's no dead body odor, so that's one positive sign."

The men figured the best way to enter the vehicles without disturbing fingerprints would be through the passenger side. When Hawkman opened the door to Destiny's car, Rochester howled pitifully and jumped inside. He had to manually lift the dog out and command him to sit. The hound reluctantly lay down at Hawkman's feet and watched with sad, droopy eyes.

After they ran a quick visual check on both cars, Hawkman took a small stick and raised the front floor mats in Destiny's car. He found the ignition keys under the driver's side. Max did the same with Carmen's vehicle and found her keys in the same spot. They didn't worry about fingerprints as they had to check the trunks. Both men held their breath as the lids popped open. Each breathed a sigh of relief when all they found were the extra tire, jack and some miscellaneous items.

Let's leave the keys where we found them, in case Williams

gets here before we do. Hawkman then turned to the guard propped against the tree. "Where are the women who were in these cars?"

The prisoner screwed up his face in a puzzled expression. "Don't know what you talk about. Women? They told me to guard cars. Make sure no one stole them. I know nothing about women."

"Who gave you your orders?"

"A man."

"What's his name?"

"Don't know. He pay me cash. Don't need name."

"So what the hell does he look like?" Max asked.

"No talk anymore. Need lawyer."

"Damn," Max said. "We'll let Williams at you."

Fear flashed in the man's eyes. "Who Williams?"

"No talk anymore," Max said, untying the cord from around the tree. He then grabbed the guard under his armpit and hoisted him to a standing position.

Hawkman untied the sentry's feet and held onto the loose end of the leash. He hooked the strap of the assault gun over his shoulder, then picked up his own rifle. "Come on, boy," he called to the hound. "Let's go home."

When the men reached the 4X4, they shoved the guard face down into the jump seat area of the king cab and again tied his feet. Hawkman gave Rochester some food and water before he dropped the tailgate to let the dog jump inside.

Worried that their prisoner might work himself loose, Max and Hawkman stowed the rifles up front. Max held his revolver to the guard's head. "Don't try anything stupid," he warned.

The man grunted and shifted his position.

Hawkman drove slowly over the rough terrain until he hit the dirt road, then picked up speed. Their prisoner moaned about the cord cutting into his wrists and his head bumping against the side.

Max poked the .45 into his face. "Shut-up and stop complaining."

Hawkman's attempts to get though to Detective Williams

on his cell phone didn't succeed until he reached the freeway. He explained the situation. "You need to get a couple of tow trucks and haul those vehicles out of there as soon as possible. They're bound to hold some clues. Once the head honcho misses his guard, he'll go out to the location and know immediately that site has been disturbed. He could either set the cars afire or move them."

"I'll get right on it. What does your prisoner report?"

"Acting dumb. Claims he knows nothing about the women or who hired him. So, you'll have to take over."

"That will give me great pleasure."

Hawkman chuckled. "We'll be there within the hour and you can have him."

He hung up and glanced at Max, who held his pistol over the seat aimed at the man. "He's awfully quiet."

Max grinned. "I can tell you he hasn't gone to sleep and his hands are still tied." He leaned his head over the seat. "You still alive, punk?"

The man groaned. "Where you taking me?"

"It's a surprise. Don't you like surprises?"

Hawkman shook his head, a smile tickling the corners of his mouth. "You haven't changed a bit."

Max thumped the seat with the butt of the gun. "This bastard makes me sick. Where does he think we're taking him? To a birthday party?" He leaned back over the seat. "We're taking you to jail, you idiot."

The man tried to raise his head. "Why? I do nothing wrong. Only doing my job."

"Don't you think it a bit odd to guard two cars out in the wilderness? Didn't you ask any questions? Did you ever engage your brain?"

"I got paid good money. I got raise when they brought in second car last week."

"That should even cause you to be more suspicious." Max hissed through gritted teeth. "Did you ever wonder why they wanted you to cover up the cars so no one would spot them?"

"Don't know."

Max sighed loudly. "You might be an accessory to murder, my friend. Nothing would make me happier than to see a numskull like you behind bars."

"I no kill anyone," the man said, his head bobbing up and down. "I never shoot gun."

Rolling his eyes, Max slumped against the seat. "God save me. I can't stand it. The man really is stupid."

They soon rolled up to the back of the police station where prisoners were unloaded. Hawkman had Williams paged. The detective appeared within a few minutes and gave orders for the prisoner to be searched, fingerprinted and put in a holding cell. He then turned to Hawkman.

"Normally, we'd wait until daybreak, but I think you're right about retrieving the cars. I have two tow trucks and the lab unit on standby. Give me the instructions on how we get there."

Hawkman scratched his chin. "Have them meet us at Exit 113 off Interstate 5. I'll have to lead the way. Otherwise, they'd never find it in the dark."

"Okay, let's hit the road."

"Would it be okay if I left Rochester here at the station."

Williams raised his brows. "Rochester?"

"Yeah, Jesse's hound. He's the one who found the cars."

CHAPTER TWENTY-THREE

Once Hawkman and Max led the authorities to the vehicles, the lab technicians set up floodlights that lit up a big part of the area. The two men took advantage of the illumination and ascended the hill where they'd seen the guard emerge. They followed a narrow, rough trail, where they came across a small wooden shack. Drawing their guns, they eased up along the edge of the building and took positions on opposite sides of the door. His gun poised, Hawkman yelled, "Anyone there?"

Receiving no response, he kicked open the door. When nothing happened, he beamed his flashlight around the interior. A rumpled sleeping bag and dirty pillow lay on top of a cot which filled one wall of the single-room shanty. In the far right corner sat a table loaded with a camper stove, a couple of pans, a few eating utensils and a kerosene lamp. A small ice chest had been scooted underneath. A couple of shelves held canned goods, peanut butter, crackers and a loaf of bread. In the corner behind the door stood a covered pot. A sack full of trash with an army of ants scurrying in and out sat next to the entry .

Hawkman strolled over to one of the two windows and peered out. "Perfect view of anyone approaching those cars. He never had to leave this place to spot an intruder."

"Livin' in the lap of luxury," Max said, as he squatted and yanked the ice chest from under the table. "Throw your light over here."

Hawkman stepped next to him and directed the beam into the container.

"This is interesting," he said, poking his finger on a piece of floating ice next to some cans of beer and soda. "I'd surmise he's made a trip into town within the last couple of days. Or else, someone is bringing him supplies."

Closing the lid, he wiped his wet fingers on his pants and pushed the chest back with his foot. He glanced at the shelves, then around the room. "Wonder where he gets his water? Don't see any bottles or buckets around."

"Could be a fresh stream nearby," Hawkman said, peering down at the stack of cooking gear. "Those pans and utensils look reasonably clean."

Max nodded. "That's possible."

Hawkman headed for the door and motioned for him to follow. "Let's search for his vehicle. I can't imagine him being up here in this isolated hell hole without some sort of wheels."

Max stepped over the threshold and sniffed the air. "It's blacker than pitch out here and I smell rain."

"I think you're right," Hawkman said, glancing skyward. "Just saw a bolt of lightning." At that moment, a clap of thunder rumbled across the sky. "We better get the hell out of here and let the detective search for the punk's vehicle."

The two men scrambled down the dark hillside. The lab unit had obviously packed up and left. When they reached the scene, the two tow trucks loaded with the girls' cars, were chugging back toward the road.

Williams brushed his hands together. "We dusted for prints on the outside and sealed up the doors because we need to get them out of here before this storm hits. We can do the inside once we have them in town." Then the detective turned and hurried toward his car. "I'm also headin' out. I don't have 4-wheel drive and I'd hate like hell to get stuck out in this god-forsaken area. See ya back in town."

Hawkman hesitated momentarily wondering if they shouldn't hunt for the guards vehicle, but doubted it would make any difference. That punk probably had no knowledge of any thing other than those two cars he'd been hired to protect.

A sudden gust of wind almost took his hat and large drops of rain pelted his face. He waved at Max. "Let's get the hell outta here."

The two men raced to the truck as the downpour hit. Hawkman drove at a rapid pace, making it to the gravel road before the ground had a chance to turn into a quagmire. They were on Interstate 5 within thirty minutes.

Max pulled a blue bandana from his pocket and wiped his face. Taking off his cloth camouflage hat, he put it on the floorboard next to the heater vent. "Man, that rain poured down in buckets. I got soaked in a matter of seconds."

Hawkman nodded. "Yeah, quite a cloudburst."

"When do you want to head back out here and find that idiot's mode of transportation?"

"I'm not so sure it's important. I think he's just a flunky hired to protect those vehicles. I doubt it's worth spending the time."

"You're probably right. But I'm glad Williams came and got those cars. He seems like an okay detective." Max lit up a cigarette. "I sure as hell hope they find some clues."

Hawkman pulled a toothpick out of his pocket. "Williams is a good man. I've worked with him on several cases and if there's any evidence inside those vehicles, his staff will find it."

"So what's your fix on this so far?" Max asked, blowing a smoke ring.

"Not sure. But I want to come back out here in the morning and explore a few of those side roads off that main drag. One of my informers told me there's a nice house hidden up in those hills that belonged to the Ricardos."

"Count me in."

By the time Hawkman dropped Max off, the rain had stopped and he headed for the police station, hoping to get in on the interrogation of the guard they'd brought down from the hills. Also, he needed to get Rochester home before Jesse thought he'd killed his dog.

Parking behind the station, Hawkman hopped out of the truck and couldn't believe his ears. It sounded like a trio of coyotes baying at the moon. He walked around the corner where two officers stood on each side of Rochester with their heads pointed upward and lips pursed. He couldn't help but laugh out loud at the sight. If only he had a camera, he could blackmail those two for the rest of their lives.

When the two officers spotted Hawkman, they immediately lowered their heads and clamped their mouths shut.

"You guys auditioning for anything in particular?" Hawkman asked. "I hate to tell you but the only one with any talent is Rochester."

The two red-faced men chuckled in embarrassment. "This hound is something else. He's kept us entertained."

"I'm not sure it isn't the other way around." Hawkman grinned. "But it's good to know the dog has been active. We've been worried about him ever since Destiny disappeared."

"Maybe we kept his mind off her," one of the officers said, reaching down and giving Rochester a pat on the head. "Understand he found her car."

Hawkman nodded. "Yeah, now to find Destiny. Could you guys keep entertaining the hound while I go see if Williams got anything out of that so-called guard?"

"Sure, no problem. It's been pretty quiet around here."

Hawkman ambled inside the holding area. "Hey, Jack, Detective Williams around?" he asked the officer manning the desk.

"He's in that second interrogation room," he said, pointing.

"Anyone using the one next to it?"

"Nope, it's empty."

Hawkman nodded and headed toward the vacant room. He stepped inside and stood at the two-way mirror where he could see Williams talking with the guard. He reached under the window area and flipped on the intercom.

"It's hard to believe, Jose Lopez, that you don't know the man's name that hired you. How did you get paid?

Jose looked like a dirty rag doll. His shirt-tail hung out in the back and his legs were sprawled under the table. It appeared he could slide off the chair and onto the floor with the least provocation. "Cash," he said, blinking his eyes. "Like I told the man with eye-patch and his mean buddy. Don't need to know a name as long as I get paid cash."

"Then who paid you and where?"

"Sometimes he come by shack in hills and other times told me to meet him at bar. One night he wanted to give me some strange stuff instead of money."

Williams raised a brow. "What do you mean? Drugs?"

Jose shook his head and raised both his hands. "No, no. Chains and handcuffs, like you use for, how you say, different type of sex."

This piqued Hawkman's interest. That must have been the night when he hid in Tony's pantry and saw him taking that stuff out. In a way it eased his mind, thinking maybe Tony wasn't using it on the girls after all.

"Did you accept them?"

"No use for that stuff. Need dollars for food and gas."

"By the way, how'd you get to that shanty in the hills. Someone take you? We didn't see a car."

"I hide motorcycle, because someone might steal it."

Hawkman figured if a dirt bike was Jose's only means of transportation, that pretty well took him off the hook as the one that shot at him. And from the other answers coming out of this flunky's mouth, he doubted very seriously that he knew anything other than he'd been hired solely to protect those cars.

Once Williams had the guy pretty relaxed, he asked. "So, only one man paid you?"

Jose held up two fingers. "Two men. Each at different times. They not come together."

"Describe them."

Jose shrugged. "Always wore dark glasses, gloves and hats."

"Were they big, little, black, Asian. Surely you could tell something about their physical appearance."

"One medium tall, other bigger. Tall man dressed nice. Other one always dirty with stringy hair."

Hawkman figured that one to be Tony. He noticed Williams' frustration as he pulled several mug shots from his pocket and slapped them on the table. As he spread them out, Hawkman craned his neck and spotted Tony Ricardo's picture in the middle of the group.

"Any of these men look familiar?" Williams asked.

Jose leaned forward. His gaze went from one picture to the next. When he came to Ricardo's, Hawkman spotted the muscles ripple at the man's jaw line, but he didn't say anything.

"Do any of these photos resemble either of the men who paid you?" Williams asked again.

Jose flopped back in the chair and clamped his hands together in his lap. He stole a quick glance at Tony's picture, then shook his head. "No."

Williams left the mug shots on the table and studied Jose's face. "When they hired you, how did these men explain the job you'd be doing?"

"Just make sure no one bothers cars."

"Why?"

Jose shrugged. "I no ask."

"Where'd you get the gun?"

"They told me everything I needed would be in the shack. That's where I found it."

"You knew how to use it?"

He nodded.

"Did they tell you to shoot any intruders?"

"No, just fire warning shot. They figured that would do it."

"When did they hire you?"

Jose scratched his head. "About month ago."

"How long did they tell you the job would last?"

He shrugged again. "Don't know. Until they don't need me no more."

"Didn't it make you wonder why they wanted the cars watched?"

"I not ask questions Only do job."

Williams thrust the picture of Ricardo toward him. "You sure you don't recognize this man?"

Jose slumped deep into the chair. His right cheek jerked with a tic and he mumbled. "I want lawyer."

"What's your lawyer's name?"

"Don't have one. No money."

The detective scooped up the pictures, slipped them into his pocket and stood. "We'll get a lawyer assigned to you as soon as possible."

Hawkman flipped off the intercom and waited until the guard had taken Jose out of the room. He then stepped into the hallway and caught up with Williams as he headed toward his office.

The detective shook his head. "I don't think the man knows much, and I doubt he realizes how much trouble he's in for guarding the missing women's cars. And he's definitely protecting Ricardo."

"Yeah, I slipped into the room next door and from what I observed got the same impression."

"Not much more we can do this evening. I'll have a lawyer assigned to him first thing in the morning."

Hawkman stopped and checked his watch. "I gotta get that dog home before Jesse thinks I've lost him. Then, first thing in the morning, Max and I are heading back out to that area, but this time without the hound. My inner sense tells me we've missed something."

CHAPTER TWENTY-FOUR

Max Pritchard took off his wet jacket and hung it over a kitchen chair to dry. He unbuckled his shoulder holster, removed the gun and placed it on the kitchen table. He then shed his damp clothes, dropping them onto the floor and ran stark naked for the shower.

With the warm water streaming over his body, he lifted his clear tenor voice to a level he thought considerate of the neighbors, but wouldn't get him evicted. He let loose with a rollicking Irish ballad that his grandfather had taught him. Crooning the final words of the song, he smiled to himself, remembering the first time Hawkman had heard him sing.

"My God, you can actually carry a tune. In fact, you sing good," he'd told him.

He liked having his old partner back alive and well. Such a shame he'd gotten injured. But he seemed to be faring fine and they were back working on a case together. Max enjoyed that feeling and it amazed him how the name Hawkman rolled off his tongue so easily, as though he'd always called him that.

He dried himself, dressed, put the dirty clothes in the washer, then sat down to clean his Colt .45. This job he could do in his sleep, so his thoughts wandered to the missing girls. He went over in his mind what he and his buddy had discovered with the help of the hound and prayed the authorities would find some clues inside those cars. If it hadn't been for Hawkman, he would never have located those vehicles on his own. Up to this point, his search for Carmen hadn't led him in the direction of the bingo halls. He'd about given her up for dead. Now he had hope and could feel his whole search energized with the discovery.

Whoever hid those vehicles had to be familiar with that section of the hills. He wondered if the girls were lured into driving to that location? Or were they driven there by the abductors? He really felt the latter to be the case. If so, then where were the women? Pulling the cleaning rod from the barrel, his hand stopped in mid-air. "Damn, they could be buried somewhere in that God forsaken area," he mumbled.

After the rains, graves would be hard to locate unless they were very shallow. Is that what Hawkman had in mind by wanting to explore those side roads? Max rocked his chair back and stared at the ceiling. No, that couldn't be it, because he'd mentioned the Ricardo's house. Knowing this agent from years back, he sensed Hawkman thought the girls were alive and being held against their will. Probably drugged. But why?

Max finished cleaning his gun and set it aside. He thought about the phone call he'd received a couple of days ago, informing him that the Agency had been looking into the theory that wealthy foreigners were hiring people or gangs to abduct women for sex slaves. As far fetched as this sounded, they told Max to keep his eyes and ears open as he searched for Carmen. He exhaled, making a hissing noise between his teeth. Hard to believe that such a crime could take place in this small town, but all the more reason they needed to find those girls fast.

❧

Hawkman picked up Rochester from the two officers and headed for Jesse's. It would be close to 9 PM by the time he arrived. The old man would pump him for every detail. He hoped Amanda would be in bed because he couldn't lie. And if the child knew her mama's car had been found, no telling what type of scenario she'd conjure up in her head.

Parking in front of the farm house, Hawkman walked to the rear of the truck and dropped the tailgate so Rochester could jump out. The dog immediately went to the porch where

Jesse had left a fresh bowl of water and food scraps. The hound gulped down the meat and lapped up some water, then plopped down on his familiar rug. He dropped his snout to his paws and looked at Hawkman with soulful eyes.

"You did a good job today," he said, rubbing the dog between his ears.

Glancing up, he spotted Jesse standing at the door.

"Been waitin' for ya."

"Sorry we're so late, but I had to attend to some stuff at the station."

"Hope that means you've got some good news."

Hawkman straightened and took a deep breath. "Yes and no." He peered over Jesse's shoulder. "Amanda around?"

"She's in bed."

"Good. Let's go inside."

He told Jesse about the events of the day and that Rochester had performed well.

"This is our first big break in the case. We're hoping the cars will hold some prints or other possible clues that will help us find the girls."

Jesse's shoulders drooped. "But still, no sign of my Destiny?"

"Sorry, Jesse. But we'll find her. I feel it." He stood and patted the old man's shoulder. "I better go so you can get to bed. By the way, that hound of yours hasn't lost his tracking ability. I may want to use him again."

"Any time."

Hawkman left Jesse's with a heavy heart. He could see the old man aging by the day. Almost home, he drove over the bridge and glanced toward his house. Something didn't seem right. Not a glimmer of light showed through the windows. Jennifer hadn't mentioned going out this evening. And if she had, surely she'd be home by now as it was close to midnight. Regardless, she always left on a lamp.

His gut tightened when he remembered the threatening call she'd received. He decided to drive by the dark house and approach on foot. Parking in the store lot and crouching close to his neighbor's redwood fence, he made his way back toward his property.

When he reached the split rail barrier around his own yard, he slid through the slats, pulled his gun, and crept up beside the garage. He looked through the window and could see his new 4X4 parked inside, but not Jennifer's van. He raced to the front entry and immediately noticed that the alarm wasn't set. Trying the door, he found it unlocked. Pushing it open a few inches, he listened for several seconds. Hearing nothing, he stepped cautiously inside. Keeping his back to the wall and his gun poised, he made his way into the living room. Feeling a cool breeze cross his face, he glanced at the sliding glass door and noticed the fluttering drapes.

Hawkman eased toward the dining area, now Jennifer's computer center, and discovered her monitor in the sleep mode. As he moved around the desk, he almost fell over her chair as it lay on its side.

Terrified, he flipped on the lights and called her name as he dashed from room to room. No sign of Jennifer. Her gun rested on the bedside table undisturbed and the rest of the house seemed untouched. The only indication of a struggle appeared at the computer area. He knew his wife would have found some method to deter the abductor, so whoever did this caught her off guard.

But how'd they escape the area without his seeing them on the road? No cars had passed coming from the lake area, and he would have definitely recognized Jennifer's van. Could it be possible that someone dropped off the perpetrator, and then he used her vehicle to escape out the back way?

He reached for his cell phone and realized he'd tossed it on the seat of the pick-up as it had gouged his waist as he drove. Hurrying to the kitchen phone, he dialed Max's number.

Tapping his fingers on the counter, he waited for several rings, and then the answering machine picked up. "Max, wake up. This is Hawkman. Pick-up. I need to talk to you. Pick-up, Max, this is an emergency."

A sleepy voice finally came on the line. "Yeah, who's this?"

"They've got Jennifer."

"Hawkman!" Max exclaimed, his voice coming alive. "They got your wife? When?"

"Sometime this evening. I just got home." How soon can you meet me at that ramp off Interstate 5?"

"As soon as I put on some clothes."

"I'm taking the back route outta here, so it might take a few minutes longer. I'll see you there."

"I'll be waiting."

Making sure he didn't disturb any possible fingerprints, Hawkman closed the slider and dropped in the broom stick that he'd cut to fit inside the runner. Dashing into the kitchen, he hit the garage door opener they kept on the window sill, grabbed the extra door key off the hook, and slid it under the outside mat. He then dashed to the 4X4 and jumped inside. When he turned on the ignition, it wouldn't start.

"Damn!" he cursed, hitting the steering wheel with the palm of his hand. "They've messed with my truck."

Leaping out, he hit the opener on the visor and slithered under the big door before it closed. Racing to his old truck parked at the grocery store, he screeched out of the lot, leaving a puff of dust behind. Turning to the left, he headed out the back way as his right hand searched blindly for the cell phone he'd tossed on the seat. His fingers clamped over the small box and he hit the memory button for Detective Williams' private line.

On the third ring a groggy voice answered. "Detective Williams."

"This is Hawkman. They've kidnapped Jennifer."

"What the hell are you talking about?"

"Jennifer's gone."

"Are you sure?"

"I arrived home late and discovered her van missing, along with evidence of a struggle in my living room. If they harm one hair on her head, I'll kill them. No questions asked."

"Where are you now?"

"I'm heading out the back way around Copco Lake. They

never came down Ager Beswick Road or I'd have seen them. Max is meeting me off Interstate 5."

"Hawkman, take it easy. You're not sure she's been kidnapped. Maybe there was an emergency."

"She'd have let me know."

"Surely they wouldn't be so dumb as to take the van to the same place where they hid the other cars. Wait until daylight."

"You know I can't do that."

A moment of silence. "Yeah, I hear ya. I'll get an All Points Bulletin out on her van immediately. Give me the information."

"You're going to have to look it up. The van is under her name, so it shouldn't be a problem."

"Okay. I'll have my lab crew out at your place first thing in the morning"

"Thanks. I've left the alarm off and a key under the doormat. Also, I need another favor. Get over to the courthouse as soon as you can and look up the Ricardo's property. I never got there. I need to know the exact location of their home before they passed away. My gut tells me that it's somewhere up in those hills where we found the cars. The listing will be under Marco and Elsa Ricardo or Tony's name. Let me know as soon as you have the information."

"The court house doesn't open until eight o'clock at the earliest."

"Offer one of the clerk's a hundred bucks to get there sooner. I'll reimburse you."

The detective let out a sigh. "I'll see what I can do."

"Thanks, Williams. I owe you one."

Hawkman snapped the phone back on his belt and paid closer attention to the rough road. In the beam of his headlights, he couldn't make out any recent tracks on the hard pan surface, but he scanned the road for any recent broken limbs or fallen foliage. He spotted a few green leaves in his path, but nothing indicated they'd been knocked off by a vehicle.

When he got to Irongate Dam, he made a quick run through the picnic areas but didn't find any sign of Jennifer's van. He drove into Hornbrook and veered off onto North Interstate 5. His tension hadn't eased and he knew the trek up to the area where they'd found Destiny's and Carmen's cars would probably be useless. But he had to try.

He took the exit off the freeway and as he rounded the corner, spotted Max's black Durango parked off to the side. The glowing tip of a cigarette signified the presence of his old buddy sitting behind the wheel.

Parking behind him, Hawkman jumped out and hurried toward the driver's side. Max rolled down the window and studied his face.

"You look like hell."

Hawkman felt like he'd been gritting his teeth for hours and tried to relax his jaw. "I'm not entering a beauty contest. Come on, let's go."

Max climbed out of his vehicle and locked it, then joined Hawkman in his pick-up.

"Do you actually think the kidnapers would come back to the area that we've already invaded?" Max asked.

"No, but they aren't too bright and I have to check."

"There must be someone who has some brains in this operation. These guys appear to be the flunkies doing the dirty work. You have any idea who it might be?"

Hawkman shook his head. "None. I can't figure out why this is happening in our small town."

"Have you had any contact with the Agency lately?"

"No one except Broadwell and I just had a check ran on you."

Max told him about the wealthy foreigners hiring gangs and stooges to find beautiful women for sex slaves.

Hawkman glanced at him, his brow furrowed. "Here?"

Max shrugged. "They told me to keep it in mind while trying to find Carmen. It's happening. Believe it or not."

"Dear God!" He gripped the steering wheel until his fingers turned white. "They could fly these women out of here and we might never find them."

❧

His face screwed in anger, the older man stood with his legs apart, fists on his hips, and glared at the two men cowering in front of him. "You did what! Can't you two stay out of trouble until we've completed this job? Why the hell didn't you come and get my approval before doing such a stupid thing. You realize what a risk you've put us in by taking Hawkman's wife? Do you know who he is?"

"Just a nosy private investigator," one of the men said in a low voice.

The older one pointed an accusing finger at the young man. "Tom Casey is not just any private investigator. Many years back he served as a top secret agent and has many contacts. Before you know it, this whole place will be swarming with Agency men."

Both younger men shrugged. "Oh, sure, we've all heard those rumors."

"This should tell you why I'm boss and you're not. It's not gossip and now you've thrown the whole operation into jeopardy by pulling this stunt."

"So what are we going to do?"

"I don't know yet. I've got to think about it." Pacing the floor, he turned to the taller of the two. "Is Jennifer with the other women?"

They both nodded.

"Hell, that takes care of letting her escape."

"How'd you transport her?"

"Took her mini-van," one of the men mumbled.

The older man slapped his forehead. "Damn!"

"Where'd you hide it? I hope to hell you didn't take it to the field."

"No. We stored it in the garage."

The elder shook his head. "Thank God, you at least had enough sense to put it out of sight." He waved his hand. "Now, get out of here and let me think."

As the two men turned to leave, he raised his forefinger. "No drinking. You might have to be ready in a matter of minutes. Carry your phones with you at all times. I want no more problems and don't do anything without my approval again. Do you think you can handle that?"

"Yes sir," they responded in unison.

When he heard the door slam, he sat down at his desk, picked up the phone and punched in 011, the international prefix code.

CHAPTER TWENTY-FIVE

After the men spent three grueling hours searching through the dark and finding nothing, Hawkman pulled up to Max's vehicle.

"Thanks, Max. I appreciate your coming out here with me. I knew in my gut it would probably be futile, but I had to try."

Max cuffed him on the shoulder. "No problem. I'd advise you to go home and get some rest. I've taken off a couple of days from work, so don't hesitate to call me." He got out, then turned back to Hawkman as he pulled a cigarette from his pack. "By the way, you still have that hand- sketched map you found in Ricardo's truck?"

"Yeah," he pointed. "It's there in the glove compartment. I never took it out. Why?"

"Mind if I take it and look it over?"

"Not at all. Hope you can come up with something. If so, let me know."

Max found the paper, stuck it in his pocket and shut the truck door.

By the time Hawkman reached home, he felt the mental strain taking over. The thoughts of losing the woman he loved so much ate at his very soul. He shed his dirty clothes, pulled his .45 from the shoulder holster and placed it on the kitchen counter. He'd clean it first thing after a bit of shut-eye. Couldn't have a malfunctioning gun for what he had in mind. Taking a hot shower, he dropped into an empty bed and tried not to think of his beautiful wife's ordeal. He knew he had to have a few hours rest and a clear mind to pursue the kidnappers.

His eyes snapped open after three hours of heavy sleep and he jumped from bed. Williams would be sending his lab guys out first thing this morning. Hawkman hoped that the detective had been able to get into the court house and would have that information too. Meanwhile, an ugly thought had run through his mind. He rushed to the computer, booted it up and went on a search.

He used some of the facilities to which only private investigators were privy, and within an hour he found some very interesting information. As he read, his gut tightened and his fury climbed. He punched the print button with force. While the data rolled out of the printer, he dressed and put on a pot of coffee. Under normal circumstances, he would have enjoyed the streaks of golden sunlight filtering across the sky as he went out to the aviary to check on Pretty Girl. But this morning his thoughts were grim and angry. How dare anyone come into his home and take his wife. The falcon flapped her wings in anticipation as he opened the screen door to the bird's cage.

"Sorry, girl. You'll have to be satisfied with man-made food again. I'm afraid Jennifer comes first."

After taking care of the falcon's needs, he gave his gun a quick cleaning, loaded it, flipped on the safety, then fastened the shoulder holster across his chest. He glanced out the kitchen window when he heard gravel crunching. Detective Williams followed the police van as they drove their vehicles up the driveway.

Hawkman met the crew at the door and ushered them inside. "Glad you made it early."

"Didn't think you'd hang around long, so thought we'd better high-tail it out here," Williams said.

Hawkman guided the technicians to the sliding glass door, and explained that he thought the intruder had entered there and caught Jennifer by surprise. The lab men immediately set to work dusting for prints.

Detective Williams strolled into the kitchen and waited

for the technicians to finish asking Hawkman questions before he called him over. "I did what you said and bribed one of the clerks to come into the courthouse early. So, you owe me a hundred bucks."

"No problem," Hawkman said, pulling five twenty dollar bills from his pocket. "I appreciate it."

The detective placed several sheets of paper on the counter. "The deed is made out with all three names: Elsa, Marco and Tony Ricardo. So the property automatically went to Tony after his folks passed away."

"That makes sense," Hawkman said, peering over William's shoulder. "I hope you got a map of the property."

"Yes." He flipped over the top sheet and pointed at the parcel number he'd circled. "It's tucked back in the woods off that main road right after it turns to gravel."

Hawkman frowned as he studied the map. "I don't recall a road near that location."

"It might just have a dirt driveway leading up to the house. And if it hasn't been used in awhile, it could well be overgrown with weeds. That area is such a dense forest that you probably wouldn't be able to spot the residence from the road."

Hawkman thought about his talk with Manette. She'd described the place as well-hidden and up among the hills. He nodded. "You've got a point."

Their attention went to one of the technicians who crawled out from underneath Jennifer's computer center holding up a small plastic bag. "This looks mighty suspicious," he said.

"What is it?" Williams asked.

"A rag that smells very much like chloroform. I'll know more when I get it back to the lab."

Hawkman gritted his teeth. "That's why she didn't put up much of a fight," he hissed. He snatched up the papers, rolled them into a tube and grasphed them in his hand. A picture flashed in his imagination of Jennifer lying in the back of her van, unconscious, duct tape across her mouth, ropes securing her wrists and ankles.

His thoughts were forced back to the present by one of the

men touching his arm. "Mr. Casey, are there other areas that you feel we should check? If your wife had to be carried to her van, I'd say they went out the front door. We might find something between here and the garage."

"Check it out," he snapped. These men had obviously been briefed by Williams. "They also did something to my 4X4 so that it won't start. Look that over too." He then turned to the detective. "I can't hang around here much longer."

Williams shot him an intense look. "What are your plans? You shouldn't try to take this on by yourself."

"I don't have much of a choice." He slammed his fist against the counter top. "I can't wait for the police department to go through all this red tape before searching for Jennifer!"

About that time, Hawkman's cell phone vibrated against his waist. He snatched it off his belt, walked out the front door and past the garage where the lab crew were working over his 4X4. "Hawkman here."

"Hello, Mr. Casey. This is Teley from the bingo hall."

"Yeah?" Hawkman said, curious as to why this man was calling.

"One of my workers has a police scanner, and heard the APB go out on Jennifer and her van."

Hawkman stopped his pacing and caught his breath. "Has someone spotted it?"

"Unfortunately, no. But we want to help you find her. My men are highly skilled. They know how to use guns."

Rubbing his forehead with his hand, Hawkman exhaled loudly. "Teley, I really appreciate your offer. But your men could get in trouble, and even be hurt. I don't want them to take that risk."

"We're aware of that and are willing to take the chance. We also know that the police might take three or more days to begin their investigation. I have a feeling you're not going to wait that long. And you can't do it alone."

Taken aback by this offer, Hawkman found himself lost for words. "Let me get back to you. I have the police here now."

"No problem," Teley said. "I'll be at the bingo hall if you want to reach me."

Hawkman hung up, his brain buzzing with the idea of a force of men to help him search the hills. It might well be something to take into consideration. He'd talk to Max and see what he thought about the proposition. New hope surged through his veins.

CHAPTER TWENTY-SIX

Hawkman stood at the garage entrance and watched the lab crew finish gathering the evidence.

One of the men glanced up. "Does your wife always park her van on the left side?"

"Yes."

"Does she pull in straight or back in?"

"Straight."

"Do you drive your wife's van often?"

Hawkman shook his head. "Very seldom. In fact, it's been over two weeks since I drove it."

"You have on cowboy boots. Is that what you usually wear?"

"Yeah. Why all the questions? Have you found something?"

"We discovered a print coming toward the garage. It appears to be some sort of work boot with crevices in the sole. It leads toward the passenger side of where your wife's vehicle would have been parked. It caught our attention because it looked recent. If the kidnapper carried her, his weight plus hers caused his feet to sink deeper into the dirt and gravel." He pointed toward the area between the house and garage where Hawkman could see the residue of the plaster they'd used. "Then, when he stepped into the garage on the concrete floor the sole made another print. We took a cast of them both. Not sure how good the one on the concrete will turn out, but at least we might be able to tell if they came from the same boot."

"Nice work," Hawkman said.

The man nodded. "We're just doing our job. Oh, by the way,

some wires were disconnected on your SUV. One of the guys reattached them and it should start right up. You might want to give it a try while we're still here in case they did something else we didn't spot."

"Thanks. Did you find any more clues besides the boot impressions?"

"Yep. A real nice whole hand print on the hood of your 4X4. Probably when he slammed it down after detaching the wires."

Hawkman climbed into his vehicle and the engine turned right over. Giving a thumbs up, he drove out of the garage and parked beside the old truck. He removed the rifles and ammunition from the jump seat area and placed them in the back seat of the 4X4. He then went back inside the house and retrieved an extra box of shells for his pistol and slipped his Buck knife inside his boot.

While the detective and his crew were packing up to leave, Hawkman went back to the bedroom and phoned Max. "You ready to hit it today?"

"Just tell me when and where."

"I'm coming into town so I'll pick you up in about an hour. Little errand I want to run before heading into the hills. I'd like you to go."

"I'll be ready," Max said.

Hawkman went into his computer room and stuffed the data he'd printed out into his pocket, then headed into the living room. Detective Williams had come back inside and stood staring out the sliding glass door.

"You sure have a beautiful view over the lake."

"Sorry, I can't enjoy it with you right now, I'm out of here."

Williams walked toward the entry, his expression grim. "You want to tell me where you're headed?"

"Nope. But I'll let you know if I come across something worthwhile," he said, picking up the map and deed off of the counter.

The detective let out a sigh and stepped out the front door. Hawkman locked up behind him, removed the key from under the doormat and set the alarm. At least if someone had any ideas about ransacking the house, they'd meet with a lot of noise.

He jumped into the 4X4, had to swerve around the lab van and Williams' unmarked car to get to the street, then headed toward Medford. When he reached Max's apartment, he found his friend waiting for him outside.

Before driving away, Hawkman showed him what he'd discovered on the internet. Max raised a brow.

"Shit! You think he's heading this operation?"

"After what you told me about the Agency's warning of a ring of thieves stealing women for sex slaves, I did some research. There's big money in it. I also went back into the history of missing women in this area. There have been several, but none of whom were locals. They were either transients or presumed to be prostitutes and the police never got involved in full investigations. From my research, it looks like this has been going on for at least a couple of years."

"That's interesting," Max said. "It appears that the buyers started complaining about their merchandise or why would the kidnappers change their modus operandi to snatching women of a higher class?"

"I'd imagine more money is at stake. But what I don't understand is this local knows I have a connection with the Agency even though he might not be sure just how. There should be no doubt in his mind that I'd use all my resources to get anyone who harmed my family. So tell me, why the hell would he take a chance and kidnap Jennifer?"

Max raised a brow. "It makes me think that the flunkies took things into their own hands. And they're not thinking Agency. They're concentrating on a nosy private investigator who's getting too close for comfort and they're going to teach you a lesson."

Hawkman hit his fist on the steering wheel. "You're probably right. But what really scares me is that Jennifer might not even be with the other women."

Max rubbed his chin. "We've got to assume she is and work from that angle."

"It terrifies me to think they could fly these women out of here before we find the hideout." Hawkman took a deep breath and started the engine. "We've got to move fast."

Before pulling into the street, he handed Max the property blueprint showing the location of Ricardo's house. Taking the hand-drawn map from his pocket, Max compared it. "Yep, it fits."

"What do you mean?"

"I studied this pencil sketch you found in Ricardo's truck and came to the conclusion that what I'd spotted might be an old driveway."

Hawkman jerked around. "Why the hell didn't you say something beforehand?"

"Because in the dark things look different. Last night, when the truck's headlights hit that area for just a split second, I thought I saw some ruts next to the road heading off into high grass and trees. Shadows can play tricks on your eyes, plus that shattered window on your old truck made it a little hard to see through. That's why I wanted to look this over." He waved the pencil sketch. "Comparing this to the property location, I think I had it right. Those depressions could be an old driveway that lead to the house. However, it looks like there's a road about a half mile past those ruts that intersects the main one which could possibly lead you to another entry at the side of the house."

Hawkman stared straight ahead and gripped the steering wheel as he thought about what the detective said about an overgrown driveway.

Max unfolded the hand sketched map and turned it over. "Probably the only reason Ricardo kept this is because he drew it on the back of a receipt from a local garage where he had some work done on his pick-up."

"Yeah, that makes sense."

"You're thinking this house might be where they have the women confined?"

Hawkman let out a disgusted sigh. "I'm not sure of anything. But we need to investigate the area today.

Max shrugged. "Hey, we've done operations like this before. It'll be a piece of cake."

"That's true. But, we usually had a couple of days or a week to plan an attack. This time we don't have the luxury of time on our side. We've got to find the women quickly, which means we may have to go in tonight. But first we'll canvass the area to determine exactly where that house is located. Once we find it and discover guards planted around the place, then we can pretty well figure something's going on."

"Yep," Max said, folding up the county map. "And if the women are there, most likely there'll be more guards inside."

"That's what worries me. It might be too dangerous for just the two of us to undertake this on our own. Yet my gut tells me we need to move swiftly or they'll whisk the girls out of there. I'm afraid we're going to need more men."

"You know the detective isn't going to give us any help unless he's sure we've got something."

"I'll definitely contact him if we suspect the women are there. But, he may not be able to supply many men on short notice."

Max slumped back against the seat. "Too bad we aren't working back in the wild west days when we could gather a posse in a few hours."

Hawkman smiled. "Bingo!"

Max shot him a look. "Huh?"

CHAPTER TWENTY-SEVEN

Jennifer's eyes fluttered open and she stared into pitch blackness. Her mouth felt so dry that she could barely swallow, and a dull headache thumped in her temples. She twisted her head back and forth trying to rise, but the weight of an elephant seemed to rest on her chest. Finding her arms free, she ran a trembling hand down her front. Two thick straps that felt like seat belts crisscrossed between her breasts and over her shoulders. They held her down tight against a mattress or pad of sorts. She traced the bindings with her fingers as far as she could and discovered the ends went over the edge and were anchored tightly under the cot beyond her reach. She tried to move her legs, but found her ankles tethered to the end of the bed.

Panic rose in her chest. She tried to remember what had happened. The last thing she recalled was a man with a ski mask suddenly coming through her sliding glass door and, before she could react, clamping a cloth over her mouth that had a pleasant odor and tasted slightly sweet.

Where was she? Her brain refused to cooperate and she fought the desire to go back to sleep. Her body tensed when she heard a low moan echo from somewhere in this black dungeon.

"Who's there?" she whispered.

"Water. I need a drink," said a raspy voice.

A door suddenly opened to her right. Jennifer squinted at the brightness from the overhead lighting that flooded the room. Her eyes quickly adjusted as she watched a person in a ski mask balance a tray of glasses filled with a clear liquid and head for a bed at the far end of the room. She studied the individual's back and from the shape of the body assumed it to be a man, but she couldn't be sure until he spoke.

"Ah, my sweet, you wanted a drink and I have brought you one. In a couple of hours I'll bring you a bite to eat."

A black slender arm reached up and took one of the glasses he offered. The man's body blocked Jennifer's view, but she had a sickening feeling in the pit of her stomach that Destiny occupied that bed.

Jennifer's head cleared rapidly and her headache eased. Her mind began to function and she wondered how he knew so quickly that the woman wanted a drink. Ah, the room must be bugged, she thought, and glanced around the walls. Sure enough a video camera hung over the door and more than likely, a speaker or intercom had been installed near by.

She watched the hooded figure cross to her left where another occupied cot sat against the wall. Jennifer could see straps going over the edges of the mattress. The form appeared to be that of a woman who had been bound to the bed in the same fashion as her.

"Wake up, pretty lady. Time for a glass of water."

The body didn't move.

Setting the tray on the floor, he gently shook her. "Come on, wake up."

Still no movement. He abruptly left the room, then returned shortly with another hooded man. As they leaned over the silent form, Jennifer heard one of them whisper. "We just got word they'll be moving them out within forty-eight hours."

Hearing those words made Jennifer's heart race. Could he be speaking about us? she wondered. Moving us to where? She listened as he spoke again.

"This woman has been here the longest. I hope she's okay and we can sober her up." He peeled back the woman's eyelids with his fingers. "I think we better walk her."

The first man reached underneath the bed and Jennifer heard a clicking noise, then the rustling sound of the restraints being pulled away. The second man flipped the covers off the woman's feet and removed the straps from around her ankles.

They scooted the female to the edge of the bed, then with a man on each side, lifted her to a standing position. The woman's knees buckled and they had to grab her before she fell to the floor.

Suddenly, she screamed, causing Jennifer to jump. "Get away from me you sons-of-a-bitch." She rotated her body in an attempt to get back into the bed. "Just let me die."

Jennifer got a good look at the girl's face and felt goose bumps rise on her arms. Even with dark circles under her eyes, a pallid complexion and puffy cheeks, she definitely resembled the picture of Carmen in Destiny's yearbook that Hawkman had shown her.

Carmen struggled to get away from the two men but they managed to keep her standing. Even though she fought them, they held on tightly and forced her to walk back and forth in the middle of the room.

One even tried talking in a consoling voice. "Take it easy. It won't be long before you'll be free."

She jerked her body backwards, spit at him and yelled obscenities. "You bastards have been telling me that for weeks." Then, she went limp in their arms, and moaned like a whipped puppy. They carried her back to the bed, replaced the straps and handed her the water. Once she gulped it down, the second man left, telling the other one to call if he needed help.

Jennifer realized these women were being drugged through water or food. Her parched mouth would have to stay dry for a while longer. The thought made her shiver and she feigned sleep when the man turned toward her. Through slit eyes she watched him approach her bed carrying the tray with the remaining glass. She could go without food, but eventually she'd have to break down and drink the water. Unless, she could figure out another way to get the precious liquid. Hawkman, where are you?

The man's voice sounded muted through the mask as he spoke. "Well, looks like another pretty lady has joined us. Bet your mouth is pretty dry. Here's a nice cool glass of water."

Jennifer didn't move. When he reached down and took

hold of her arm, she brought it up in a swift movement and hit the tray he'd balanced on his other hand. It hit the floor with a bang and the glass broke into several pieces, splashing liquid across the floor.

Acting groggy, she slurred. "I need to go pee. Someone, help me up."

The man cursed under his breath, "Bitch." Then knelt to clean up the mess. "Hold on. I'll get help."

The noise must have resounded throughout the house, because two hooded men dashed into the room with guns drawn.

"What's the problem?" one said.

"She's coming out of sedation and hit the tray," he said in disgust. "Get Helen in here, this woman needs to go to the pot."

Lowering their guns, they left the room and one of them yelled, "Helen, you're needed in here."

He then picked up the broken glass, collected the other two and left with the tray.

Jennifer studied the room and noted that heavy drapes covered the walls, hiding the windows, so she had no idea whether it was daytime or night. The only furniture consisted of the three cots, a small table scooted into a corner and two straight back chairs on each side of the door.

Soon, a woman wearing a white hood, dress and shoes entered the room. She had a slight, but firm build and reminded Jennifer of a nurse. Marching straight to her bedside, she announced in a low but commanding voice, "Okay, let's get you to the bathroom."

She untied the tethers around Jennifer's ankles, then reached under the bed and fumbled with the straps.

"Damn these fasteners," she muttered.

Finally, Jennifer heard the click and the tension eased across her chest. Knowing she had to act the part, she swayed as the woman, stronger than she looked, practically lifted her to a standing position.

"Which way?" Jennifer slurred.

Helen looped a strong arm around Jennifer's armpits and guided her toward a small door on the opposite side of the room.

"Here we are," she said.

The lavatory consisted of a toilet, basin and bathtub with a plastic curtain shoved to one side. But no window graced the walls. Some air movement came from an overhead fan that squealed noisily when Helen flipped on the light. A cracked, oak trimmed mirror hung above the sink. Several dirty towels and wash cloths were slung over aluminum rods attached to the wall.

She grabbed the rim of the sink as Helen sat down on the edge of the tub. Frowning, Jennifer glared at her. "I'd like a little privacy."

"Sorry," I have to stay in here."

"Why? You think I'm going to run away? I don't even know where I am or why I'm here. Do you?"

The hooded head moved slowly back and forth. "Nope. I'm only hired to make sure your female needs are handled properly. Now get on with your business before the big boys wonder what we're doing in here."

Jennifer took care of her personal needs, then washed her hands. She cringed when she glanced in the mirror and saw a face she hardly recognized. Immediately, she released the band around her pony tail and combed her fingers through her hair, then tied it back. Cupping her hands, she filled them with water and splashed it onto her face, gulping a few mouthfuls of the liquid. At least she knew she wouldn't die of dehydration if she could just get to the bathroom several times a day.

Helen handed her one of the towels. "Okay," You look as good as can be expected. Let's get you back to bed."

"I don't want to lie down. I'm stiff and would rather walk."

Shaking her head, Helen took hold of her arm. "Sorry, those are the rules."

"Whose rules?"

"You ask too many questions," she said, guiding Jennifer

roughly back to her cot. "I wouldn't advise you to give any trouble. Those men outside this room can be mighty mean and could rough you up pretty bad if you don't obey them."

Jennifer believed her. She wouldn't have a prayer at trying to escape in her weakened condition, especially with the three men she'd already seen, this woman and who knows how many more inside the house. Plus, she could rest assured there were guards lurking outside.

As Helen tightened the straps around her chest and tied her ankles, Jennifer wondered what would happen next. Had Destiny or Carmen been raped or mistreated? But from what she'd read, rapists usually dump their victims after the abuse, or in extreme cases murder them. Since the girls were still alive, that obviously hadn't happened here. Something else must be going on. In the girls' drugged state, she might never get an answer and didn't dare ask with the room being bugged.

She'd read a novel recently by an American teacher living near Venice. The author had based her story on true accounts of criminals who persuaded destitute women from Russia and eastern Europe to travel to Italy with promises of jobs. Once in Italy, however, the women were forced into prostitution and threatened with death or expulsion back to their lives of poverty if they resisted.

Could she, Destiny and Carmen be faced with similar circumstances? Surely, nothing like that would actually happen in the United States. She shuddered. But what if it did? Where would they be taken? Would she ever see her wonderful Hawkman again? What if something terrible happened before he found her?

Helen turned off the light, pitching the room into total darkness except for the red blinking light of the video camera above the door. Warm tears slid down Jennifer's cheeks and the terror she'd managed to hold at bay surged over her. Her lips trembled and a silent voice in her brain cried out, Hawkman, I love you. Please find us quickly. A moan she couldn't stop escaped her lips and she sucked in several deep breaths to quiet her sobs.

CHAPTER TWENTY-EIGHT

When Hawkman turned the 4X4 toward the city limits going in the opposite direction, Max raised his brows. "Hey buddy, aren't we driving the wrong way to find the Ricardo house?"

"Remember, I told you I wanted to check on one more bit of business before we headed out. If my theory is right, I might have the ringleaders of this operation pegged."

"Be nice if you'd clue me in since we're supposed to be working as partners."

"Thought you'd have it figured out by now," Hawkman jested.

Max raised a finger in the air. "I'm sure I'm close, but need your input to verify my conclusion."

"When I got shot at the other night, I spotted a Toyota 4-Runner coming down off a partial road near the lake, but couldn't get close enough to read the plates. It dawned on me that I'd seen that vehicle before. I racked my brain trying to figure out where. The last place I'd seen a bunch of cars was out at the Alexander ranch. There were several vehicles parked around the garage area, but I didn't pay that much attention to their makes or models. Today, I want to check it out. It'll only take us a few minutes."

"You think that old man is going to let you rummage around his place?"

"I don't plan on asking permission," Hawkman snickered.

Max smiled as he unbuttoned his camouflage jacket so he could reach his gun easily. "I like your way of thinking."

"I'm going to journey up the driveway, pass the house,

and go right to the garage without stopping. So keep your eyes peeled and look for a white or light colored 4-Runner."

"Got it. Piece of cake."

"Right. Unless we get shot at."

Max patted his chest. "I'm ready for that, too."

They soon reached the road leading up to the Alexander ranch. Hawkman shot a stern glance at Max. "You ready?"

"Ready as I'll ever be." He pulled his gun and rested the barrel on his knee.

Hawkman turned in between the two gate pillars and drove slowly. Not spotting any activity around the main house, he followed the curve of the driveway toward the out building. The ranch appeared deserted except for the barking of the caged hunting dogs and the sound of a tractor working in one of the adjacent fields.

"I don't see anyone or a vehicle that resembles a 4-Runner," Max said, scanning the area around the back of the house. "Mostly farm machinery."

The big doors of the garage were shut, so Hawkman pulled behind it and pointed to a couple of small windows. Leaving the engine running, he shoved the gear shift into park. "Cover me," he said, jumping out.

He ran to the first glass, shaded his face with his hands and peered into the building. Unable to see the far corner, he dashed to the other window.

Meantime, Max watched the front of the house. He rolled down the window and called. "Someone's coming."

Hawkman leaped back into the 4X4, threw it into gear and gunned the engine. "Where?"

Max pointed. "You can see the dirt cloud being kicked up in the distance."

Hawkman sped down the driveway and made it onto the main road just as the vehicle crested the small hill.

"That's Roland Alexander's red sports car." Hawkman said.

"You think he recognized you?"

"I'm sure he did. It'll just make him wonder whether I came from his dad's place or Jesse's."

"Tell me, did you spot anything in the garage?"

"Yep. The 4-Runner is sitting in the corner, partially covered with a tarp. Looks like they aren't going to be using it for awhile." Hawkman narrowed his gaze toward the road and gripped the steering wheel "If any of those bastards has laid a hand on my Jennifer, I'll kill them one at a time."

Max patted his shoulder. "Don't worry. I'll help you. Now, let's go find those women."

"I'm making one more stop at the bingo parlor."

Max furrowed his brow. "What the hell?"

"I'm gonna alert my posse."

Rolling his eyes, Max flopped back on the seat. "I think you've lost it."

When they pulled up in front of the White Oaks Bingo Hall, Hawkman motioned for Max to get out. "Come meet my gang."

Max lumbered in behind Hawkman. Teley stood at the head of a table talking to several seated men. He glanced up and smiled. "I had a feeling you'd come by. So I called the men in to talk about the situation. We've all agreed to be at your command if you need us."

Hawkman stood at the opposite end of the table, his arms folded across his chest. "I appreciate this very much. I'm still not sure about anything yet." He gestured toward Max. "I'd like you to meet my partner, Max Pritchard. We're leaving right now to canvass the area where we suspect the women are being held. If we're correct and the place is heavily guarded, there's no way we can get the women out alone. That's where you'll come in."

The men nodded.

"We're ready," Argy said.

"The operation has to take place quickly under the cover of darkness tonight. You'll need to roll out of here with your weapons and in camouflage gear as soon as the sun goes down."

"That suits us fine," Elvis said.

Hawkman glanced around the room. "So who will run your bingo?"

Teley raised a hand. "Don't worry, we're covered. We have older men who couldn't handle this type of fray and women who've agreed to help."

"Do your wives know that you're about to engage in a dangerous undertaking?"

Teley looked into Hawkman's face. "Yes, Mr. Casey. They would like to go with us. We have many brave women in our group who aren't afraid of danger and know how to use a gun. They don't like the rumors they've heard. Our women want the kidnapping and trafficking of women stopped. They fear for themselves and their daughters."

"Obviously, the news is traveling fast. That's why we have to find the women tonight. We may not have a chance to save them if we wait any longer."

"Just give the word and we'll be there."

Max scratched his head when they got into the 4X4. "My God, I can't believe this. Are all these men immigrants to our country?"

"Yep."

"And they're willing to get into this mess?"

"Sure sounds like it."

Max shook his head. "I'd say they're a mighty tough breed."

Hawkman nodded as he gunned the engine and headed for Interstate 5. "It's hard to believe that they're willing to take the risks. Offering their services regardless of the consequences."

"They're all built like football players."

"Make that soccer players," Hawkman said, grinning as he turned off the freeway exit. "I think our best bet would be to go up the old driveway on foot. No one will be expecting visitors coming from that direction."

"Sounds like a good plan."

He went slowly along the road so Max could find the rut

imprints. Once he spotted them, Hawkman drove past about fifty yards and parked on the shoulder. They climbed out of the 4X4 and Hawkman replaced his leather cowboy hat with a camouflage one. Each took a rifle off the back seat and loaded it.

They hiked back up the road, scanning the area with acute awareness.

"Wonder if they have dogs guarding the area?" Max asked.

"I doubt it as there are homes around. If some kid wandered into the range of their surveillance and a dog attacked him, they'd not only get unwanted attention but lots of other trouble to boot."

"Yeah, makes sense. Why do you keep craning your neck around? Do you see something?"

"Not yet. I'm looking for a helicopter pad. I figure they'll fly the women out of here. So there's bound to be a landing spot close-by."

"Wait until we get within view of the house. They probably have a place right there. Even a small flat roof would work as some of those aircraft can practically land on a dime."

They soon reached the area of the overgrown driveway. "Okay, let's stick together," Hawkman whispered, as they followed the weed filled ruts with carefully planted footsteps.

CHAPTER TWENTY-NINE

The dense brush made it hard to identify the direction of the ruts. The furrows zig-zagged up the hill, probably made that way on purpose due to the severe winters when no vehicle could possibly make it up a straight icy incline.

"This is definitely an old driveway." Max whispered. "It's like an overgrown weed patch and there's no indication its been used recently."

Hawkman nodded. "With all these curves, this must have been a bugger to traverse in its day. We'll definitely check that other road shown on the map before we leave."

They fought the vegetation for a good hundred yards, then Hawkman put a finger to his lips and stepped behind a large oak tree. Max joined him and squinted into the sun toward the direction he pointed.

"Look near the top of the hill between those two tall trees. Doesn't that look like the tip of a roof?" Hawkman asked, keeping his voice low.

Max nodded. "Yeah. I think you're correct. Damn, no way that place could ever be seen from the road. It's completely hidden by all that foliage."

"Perfect hiding place," Hawkman hissed between gritted teeth. "We'll get a little closer, climb a tree and see what we find with our binoculars."

Crouching behind some low brush, the two men silently made their way toward the house. As they approached the dwelling, they could see the whole roof and the sun glinting off the tops of windows. Hawkman raised his hand and moved toward a stand of tall oaks. Wiping the sweat off his face with the back of his arm, he slung the rifle strap over his shoulder. He grabbed one of the lower branches and hoisted himself upward. Max went to the next tree and started climbing.

Soon, both men were as high as they could get without risking a fall. Once they balanced their bodies on a sturdy limb, they put the binoculars to their eyes.

Thinking about Jennifer, Hawkman focused on the building. From his perch, he could almost see the whole side wall of the house except for a section blocked by a couple of very mature oak trees. He spotted an entry at the far left, which appeared to be the front door. Several windows faced him. Odd, he thought. Curtains on some, but two were blacked out.

He lowered the binoculars and stared at the covered portals. "You're in that dark room, aren't you, Jennifer? I feel it," he whispered. His jaw tightened and he put the glasses back to his face. He arched his back as he spotted a cloud of dust rising from behind the house. Training his glasses on the area, he ground his teeth as he got a glimpse of a red sports car traveling rapidly up a road .

Hawkman whistled a bird call, a signal he and Max had used many times while working together. When he had his partner's attention, he pointed toward the left. They watched the vehicle skid to a stop in front of the house. Three men jumped out and disappeared inside.

Shortly, Max pointed to the far right. Hawkman raised his binoculars and spotted two males on the top of a flat roofed building. They were removing a stack of boards by throwing them over the side, then they picked up a couple of brooms and started sweeping the roof. A perfect spot for a helicopter to land, Hawkman thought.

He continued to scope the area and discovered another pair of men with rifles strapped to their backs pacing in front of the house. Max signaled again and pointed left. Hawkman swung his lens around and saw two more armed men, guarding that end. He assumed there would also be two on the back side. How many guards were inside remained a question. He now had no doubts that the women were being held in that house.

They would definitely need Teley's men to take care of the watchmen.

It worried Hawkman that they appeared to be preparing a landing pad. Did that mean they were planning on taking the hostages out immediately? That meant they'd have to manage the rescue before dark.

If Jennifer was in that house with the other two females, she could be whisked out of his life within the next few hours. His heart thumped.

Resting the field glasses on his chest, he stared at the flat topped building. No way would he leave now. He'd send Max into town to bring back the volunteers.

A plan formed in his mind. If he got close enough to that building, he could disable a helicopter with his rifle. But if it crashed and burned, the risk of the house and forest catching on fire would be great. His best bet would be to wait until it landed and take out the pilot.

He whistled again for Max and pointed toward the ground. The two descended and found a secluded area surrounded by low brush where they could discuss what they'd observed.

"I counted six guards and there's probably two on the other side," Max said. "Looks like they're staying pretty close to the house. I didn't spot any men deeper in the woods."

"Me neither. But who knows how many are inside watching the women, plus the three men who just arrived"

"Did you recognize them?"

"Old man Alexander, his son, Roland and Tony Ricardo," Hawkman said harshly.

"You were right to investigate that old man. He lost a bundle in the stock market, but made everyone believe he'd made a killing. Instead, he's raking in the bucks by kidnapping beautiful women and flying them out to wealthy foreigners." Max spit to the side. "What a sleazy ball."

"We'll tend to them later. Our first concern is getting the women to safety." Hawkman took a deep breath and glanced away. "Appears they're preparing that roof for a copter to land. They must have gotten word to move them out. One of us has to stay in case that aircraft arrives in the next few hours. We can't let it leave!"

Max wiped the sweat from his face with the corner of the green bandana he had around his neck. "They're taking a big gamble if they bring that sucker in here during daylight hours. It'll draw lots of attention as it has to be big enough to carry the three women, a couple of lookouts and the pilot."

"I'm not taking a chance. I'm staying," Hawkman said, handing Max the keys to his 4X4. "I couldn't stand to leave thinking Jennifer might be inside. Go get the men from the hall. Make sure that each one has a knife and several short pieces of rope or cord. Instruct them not to use their guns unless absolutely necessary. Give them a quick briefing on the lay of the land and have them work in twos. Teach them the bird whistle. We'll need a signal to keep track of everyone. Before you take off, drive down to that next cut off, make a right and see if you can spot that road that comes up to the house. It would save time if you could bring them up that way."

"Will do." Before Max turned to leave, he held out his rifle. "You want this?"

"No thanks, mine is enough, along with my pistol and knife. It would just drag me down. Anyway, you'll need it later and you might not be able to find me."

Max cuffed his shoulder. "Okay, buddy, be careful. I'll be back soon."

The two men parted.

Since the sun had moved directly overhead, Hawkman stayed within the trees and took advantage of their shadows to hide his movements. Even though a cool breeze rustled through the leaves, he felt sweat trickling down his back. He flipped up his eye-patch and wiped his face with the back of his sleeve.

He soon found himself close enough to the house to hear the men's voices from the roof, but couldn't make out what they were saying. He squatted down in the midst of a thatch of berry bushes.

There were two other guards in this vicinity and he needed to locate them before proceeding any closer. He soon heard footsteps on the gravel that surrounded the house. Moving a branch slightly with his hands, he spotted the legs and boots of two men not more than ten yards away. They were harassing the guys on the roof to hurry up, saying they were tired of covering two beats. The men seemed relaxed, and oblivious to the fact that they were being watched.

Hawkman calculated that it would be close to three hours before Max returned with the posse. He'd speculated on everything, including the fact that the Alexanders were the ringleaders, and the two women they'd kidnapped were being held at Tony's house. Things appeared to be falling into place.

But what if Jennifer hadn't been taken by this bunch? His heart squeezed at the thought of spending all this time following these leads if she wasn't even here. He had to know for sure.

☙

Strapped down on her back, Jennifer had wiggled so much trying to relieve the aches from the uncomfortable position that her elbows and heels felt as if they were rubbed raw.

She'd watched Helen and one of the men walk Destiny and Carmen for what seemed like hours and thought it odd they'd left her alone. Realizing they were trying to get those two out of a drugged state, she wondered, why now? Unless they really were going to move them. But where? Her heart raced when she thought about what she'd overhead from the two men earlier. They'd said something about forty-eight hours. She shivered when she recalled that story she'd read. Would they actually take them out of the country? The prospect of such a thing sent terror through her soul.

Destiny stared blankly at Jennifer several times when Helen walked her past the bed. The third time, she jerked her head around with recognition registering in her expression. Jennifer put a finger to her lips and tried to give her a smile of reassurance that she didn't really feel herself. The more she thought about their dilemma, the more she had to force herself to control panic that surged through her body.

"Why aren't you walking her?" Destiny asked, pointing at Jennifer.

"She doesn't need it," Helen snapped. "Just be quiet and keep up the pace."

Suddenly, loud male voices erupted from somewhere in the house.

"I don't want to hear any more about money. You'll get what's coming to you when I get paid."

"Yeah, when will that be? When hell freezes over? I need it now!"

Something banged against the wall, making Helen stop in her tracks and glance at the door. Jennifer could only see the woman's eyes through the ski mask and she swore she saw a flicker of fear.

"What made that noise?" Jennifer asked.

Her question jolted Helen and she glanced her way. "Probably just a chair fell over. These men get a bit boisterous."

"I thought I heard a car drive up earlier."

Helen walked Destiny to her cot and had her lay down. "You're hearing things. Just shut up and be quiet."

When she stood from locking the bands underneath Destiny's bed, she arched her back and groaned. "I need a break. I'll be back in a few minutes." She pointed at Carmen. "Be ready to take a stroll."

"Like hell I will," Carmen hissed.

Jennifer wanted to talk to the girls, but she glanced at the video camera and saw the small red light flickering. She bet that the intercom would be activated too, and would blast anything she said to ears in the other room. Feeling helpless, she let out a sigh, dreading what might happen next.

CHAPTER THIRTY

Max unlocked the 4X4, jumped inside and lit up a cigarette. He figured it would be his last for a few hours. One didn't smoke in the field unless he wanted to die. The glow from the tip marked a perfect target: right through the mouth. He shuddered when he thought of his last victim. That's exactly what gave away his position.

Before leaving for Medford, he drove down to the first intersection and made a right. He calculated that in less than half a mile he'd find the turnoff leading toward the house. Sure enough, he spotted a fairly new graded dirt driveway and noted a mailbox marked 'Ricardo' at the edge of the road.

That's all Max needed to see. Making a U-turn, he headed for the freeway. He had a gut feeling that his partner would find a way to get inside the house by the time he returned.

Once on the Interstate, he pushed his luck and drove over the the speed limit, figuring he could always show his badge if he got stopped. It took close to thirty minutes to reach the White Oaks Bingo hall and when he entered the building, many of the customers were already gathered inside. He noticed their paraphernalia of good luck pieces and daubers strewn across the tables.

Max spotted Teley in the office area and stuck his head through the window. "We need you guys now. Something's come up and the operation needs to move fast."

Several of the men gathered around. "Where's Mr. Casey?" Teley asked.

Max frowned, then his eyes brightened. "Oh, you mean Hawkman. He stayed there to keep a check on things."

The men immediately broke away and started outside. "Let's get rolling."

Teley took a moment to give instructions to the volunteers, then followed the group to one of the vehicles where they'd packed their camouflage gear. Max noticed how each man had prepared his outfit just like Hawkman wanted: short cords, knives and several other hand weapons hanging from their belts. Max rubbed his chin. "You guys look like you've been through this before."

Argy laughed. "How you think we get to America? No one send us a chartered plane."

Max eyed the men with a new appreciation. They'd do just fine. He showed them the property map Hawkman had acquired from Detective Williams, and then gave a quick verbal layout of how the house sat on the property. Then he went into how many guards they'd spotted on the outside. "We have no idea how many are inside or where they're holding the women. My hunch is that Hawkman will try to find out before we get there. It also appears that they're preparing a helicopter landing pad on the flat roof of an out-building, which indicates they plan on taking the women out of there shortly. We figure the aircraft will make its approach and land under the cover of darkness. Hawkman didn't want to take the chance they might bring it in earlier. That's one of the reasons he stayed behind. We'd like you to split up in pairs and approach the house from all angles. Don't use your guns unless absolutely necessary."

The men nodded in approval.

Max explained what they wanted done, then taught them the bird whistle signal. "This will help us keep track of each other."

After each man had mastered the call, he glanced over the group. "I think that's about it. Any questions?"

Satisfied that they all understood the procedure, he had three of the men ride with him in Hawkman's vehicle and Teley took his SUV carrying the other three. Eight men including himself. Perfect, Max thought as he started the 4X4 and led the way. They arrived at the site just as the sun dipped behind the hills. The shadows were long and the darkness under the trees made for perfect cover.

Max parked about a block away from the new driveway. Teley made a U-turn and stopped on the opposite side. The men disembarked with assorted assault rifles and were already paired up.

Teley glanced at Max. "Looks like you're stuck with me."

"No problem," he said. hauling out his gun and slinging the strap over his shoulder.

Hawkman's camouflage outerwear blended into the surrounding brush, making him almost invisible. From his hiding spot, he had a good view of the two guards making passes around the house and could easily see the two overhead on the roof. He timed the patrolling guards as to how long it took them to cover the side of the house, then swing to the back and return.

He observed the men on the roof setting up small light fixtures around the perimeter, bracing them so the rays would point skyward. This indicated to Hawkman that the helicopter would set down in the dark, guided by the beams. Hopefully, Max would be back with the posse by the time that event took place. This eased his mind a bit. But once the men on the roof were through, they'd climb down and take over their guard positions. He'd have to make a move to get into the house before that happened.

The flat roofed building, separate from the house, had two large doors on this side, which indicated that it could serve as a garage or a storage building. But the weeds that had sprouted around the front and a couple of rusted padlocks indicated it probably hadn't been used for some time.

A door from the house faced in this direction and he figured that's the way they'd bring the women out. He wondered how they planned on getting them to the rooftop. If the girls were drugged, they'd have to be carried or hoisted up in a stretcher device. He didn't see anything rigged up for that procedure. Either way, time was on his side.

The men above him appeared to be almost finished and were standing in the center of the roof surveying their handiwork. The two guards on the ground had just moved to the other side of the house. He'd better start thinking about making his move now. He calculated that he had about three to five minutes to get from his hiding place to the garage without being seen.

Hawkman slipped out of a small cave made of bushes and kept his eye on the roof workers. When both men turned their backs, he made a dash toward the building. He pressed himself against the wall, the overhang protecting him from being seen by those above. However, the other guards would be back within minutes and he needed to get out of sight. He heard one of the men on the roof instruct the other to go down and plug in the lights so he could check them out.

Hawkman's heart pounded as he realized he couldn't stay here in full view, and he didn't dare run for the house. He eased around the corner into the space between the two buildings and still saw no sign of how the men got up there. The ladder or rope must be on the far side. Suddenly, the end of an electrical cord flew over the eaves, falling not more than five feet away.

Glancing around for a means of escape, Hawkman grabbed the knob on a windowed door going into the garage. It turned easily under his grip and he quickly slipped inside, then gently closed the door.

Within seconds he heard heavy footsteps approaching and a harsh voice asking about the plug-in.

"Hell, I don't know. Look around," the voice yelled from above.

Hawkman had to hide quickly, as more than likely the outlet would be inside this room. He turned abruptly and almost ran smack dab into Jennifer's mini-van. His pulse quickened as he slipped around the front end and crouched down. The discovery of her vehicle verified that she was a prisoner in that house

The door abruptly opened. A man with a brown camouflage

hat with loose ear flaps flopping in the breeze, mumbled obscenities as he slid his hand up and down the wall next to the door. A fluorescent light hanging from the center of the ceiling fluttered awake, filling the room with a dim light. Hawkman silently eased back farther into the shadows.

CHAPTER THIRTY-ONE

Hawkman crouched behind the vehicle and quietly leaned his rifle against the wall at his back. He then slid the buck knife out of his boot and grasped it firmly in his hand. The smell of damp wood and mildew invaded his nostrils. It seemed like hours before he finally heard any noise from the outside.

"Not enough cord to reach the plug," the man yelled.

"Hold on a minute, it's snagged on one of the lights," came the voice from the roof.

"Okay, got it."

The sound of a boot crunching onto the concrete floor caused Hawkman to tense and grip his knife as the guard stepped inside the garage.

"Ah, here we go," the man grunted. "Are they working?" he called loudly.

"Yep. Perfect. All the lights are lit."

"Should I unplug 'em?"

"Naw, it's gettin' dark. Leave 'em on."

The interior light went off and Hawkman could hear the door scraping across the floor as the man pulled it partially closed. He breathed a sigh of relief and returned the knife to his boot. Staying hidden, he gripped his rifle as he listened to the echo of footsteps clunking across the roof.

"We'll leave the ladder here," the voice said. "No sense in having to set it up again."

Hawkman stepped out from behind the vehicle so he could see through the dirty window. A man sporting a brown, hard safari type hat joined the other. He continued talking as he picked up the extra length of electric cord lying on the ground and rolled it around his hand. When the hard hat fellow glanced toward the window, Hawkman stepped back, hoping he couldn't be seen.

"Gotta get this outta the way," he said, reaching up and hooking it on something above the door frame.

"'Bout time you bastards finished," a voice sneered in the background. "Took ya long enough. Now you can get back to work and do your real job so we can relax a bit."

"Ah, you're just jealous cause you didn't get the order to fix the lights," retorted the man with the floppy eared cap.

Hawkman watched as the man wearing the hard hat crossed the space between the buildings and opened the door leading into the house. He reached inside and brought out two assault rifles, tossing one to his buddy.

"Guess we better get to guardin' again," he said.

"Yeah, don't want to hear any more out of the cry-babies," the other one snickered.

Good, Hawkman thought, the door to the house is unlocked. He edged closer to the window and eyed the men in their untied combat boots as they slowly trod toward the backyard.

Wondering where the other two guards had gone, he looked through the crack in the door in the opposite direction. He wanted to make sure that both sets of men were out of sight before he made the dash across the gap between the buildings.

Standing beside Hawkman's SUV, Max pointed out the directions as he gave the men their final instructions. He and Teley would take the back, Argy and Fred, the front, Elvis and Ralph, the side area by the garage and the other two men would stay close to the road.

"Hawkman and I observed guards patrolling each side of the house. They tended to stay near the building, but be wary, there could be more out there. They work in pairs, so you'll have quite a job getting both down at once without one of you getting hurt. Use the whistle to let us know the way is clear and a variation of the signal if you get into trouble. Once we've got the guards taken care of, we'll wait for Hawkman's cue. Then we'll approach the house. "

Darkness had come and the posse crept up the road. They soon disappeared into the woods and silence fell. Since Max hadn't observed the back of the house, he needed a few minutes to get a fix on things and figure out a strategy.

He motioned for Teley and they climbed the small hill where a thick row of trees separated them from the view of the guards. As they approached the house, Max noted the red sports car still parked in front and assumed the big wigs had stayed for the climactic moment of moving out the women. He snickered to himself. What a finale they're gonna get.

He sure didn't like that flood light glaring off the back porch. It lit up the whole yard. And that damn garage roof sparkled like a Christmas tree. He'd put out those babies as soon as they took care of the watchmen.

Teley squatted behind a stand of oleanders and motioned for Max. He pointed below him where the two men were leisurely walking their route.

"They're too close to the house and right out in that bright light. We need to lure them over into those shadows," he whispered and pointed a little past the garage.

Max shook his head and kept his voice low. "Too risky. We might run into the other two guards. What we need to do is take out that floodlight. The place is lit up like a parking lot."

Teley grinned and pulled a sling shot from his back pocket.

Max looked at him in amazement. "Are you good with that thing?"

"The best. Just tell me when."

He put a hand on Teley's shoulder. "First, we need to move down closer. Let those two guys cross over toward the garage. Then, as soon as they head back and are right in front of us, blow the light."

Teley gave him the thumbs up. As the two lookouts meandered off toward the garage, Max and Teley made their way down the hill. Max found a clump of thick bushes where they were well-hidden and on the same level as the house. They'd no more settled down, ready to make their move, when a bird song echoed through the air. Teley glanced at Max and smiled. "Argy and Fred have cleared the front."

Max cuffed his shoulder. "Good show. Now, let's clean up our area."

Soon the two guards made their way back, chatting and smoking cigarettes. Teley waited until they were directly in front of him before he sailed a rock through the air. Both men jerked toward the loud shattering pop, throwing their cigarettes to the ground as darkness enveloped the back yard. Max and Teley leaped forward, looping ropes tightly around the guards' necks before they could yelp. Once the thugs lost consciousness, they were gagged, tied and dragged deep into the woods where they were secured to a tree trunk. Max unloaded their assault rifles and hid them in the shadows, then put the ammunition clips into his pocket. Teley gave Max the high sign and whistled like a bird.

Hawkman eased out the garage door and heard the first signal from the front area. Then the back area went dark and he heard the second whistle. He didn't move, hoping to hear the rest and within a few moments bird calls resonated from opposite directions. Smiling to himself, he reached inside the garage where he'd spotted the plug and gave it a yank, pitching the roof into total darkness.

Now, only a single glow came from the front porch of the house. No helicopter would risk coming down in a wooded area to an obscured pad. He stepped out into the passageway between the two buildings, emitted a shrill bird signal that echoed through the air, then reached for the doorknob leading into the house.

CHAPTER THIRTY-TWO

Jennifer squirmed in her bed as she watched Helen pace back and forth, first with Destiny and now Carmen. "Can I take a walk?" she asked. "I'm getting bedsores."

Helen let out a sigh. "Oh, all right. I'll take you in a minute."

After the woman secured Carmen back on her cot, the girl clutched her head with both hands. "I have such a horrible headache. Please, let me have some aspirin."

"It'll go away soon. Can't give you anything."

Arching her back, Helen moved to Jennifer's side. "Okay, girl, I'm going to take you for a short walk. But you don't need it like these other two."

"Are you saying I'm not full of drugs?"

"Enough," Helen said, untying Jennifer's ankles. Groaning, she reached under the bed and unfastened the straps. She then took a hold of Jennifer's arm and helped her into a standing position.

After a few minutes of parading in the middle of the room, Jennifer pulled away from the nurse's grip and proceeded to move her arms in a circular motion. She then twisted her body from side to side. "I feel stiff all over." As she bent over to touch her toes, she thought she heard the muffled sound of bird calls coming from the outside. When she straightened to a standing position, she glanced at the nurse to see her reaction. But the woman seemed oblivious to anything other than what went on directly around her.

"Okay, that's enough," Helen said, taking Jennifer's arm again and leading her toward the cot. "I'm not worried about you. Have to get these other two girls' heads clear within the next couple of hours."

Jennifer shot her a look as she sat down on the edge of the bed. "Why?"

"They're taking you out of here tonight."

When Helen attempted to lift Jennifer's legs to the mattress, she yanked them away. "Who is taking us where?"

"You ask too many questions," the woman barked. "Now, get your feet up here or I'll have to call one of the men."

Reluctantly, Jennifer hoisted them upon the bed and let the nurse tie her ankles. But when Helen struggled with the straps across her chest, Jennifer raised her body so the bands wouldn't be so tight. Helen proved to be stronger, for she yanked the binding back to where it belonged.

Again, Jennifer heard another obscure bird call, this time coming from the back of the house. Hawkman had told her stories about the Agency and how they'd used different coded whistles to identify their whereabouts. Her hopes soared.

She soon heard two more calls within minutes of each other. But when she heard the familiar whistle that Hawkman used when summoning Pretty Girl to land on his arm, her heart thumped wildly. They were going to be rescued. She felt the warm tears of relief slide out of the corners of her eyes, down her temples and into her hair.

When Max heard the signal to surround the house, he directed Teley to cover the back. He headed for the corridor between the two buildings where he figured Hawkman would enter. He moved into the passageway just as Elvis and Ralph edged around the corner of the garage. Max told one to guard this entry and the other to keep an eye on Teley in case he needed help.

Cautiously, Max opened the door to the house and stepped inside, only to meet the barrel of a rifle pointing at his chest. Hawkman immediately lowered his gun, then put his finger to his lips and waved him to follow.

Their weapons poised in an upward position, they slowly made their way down a long, dark hallway, pressing an ear to each closed door. As they approached the end, Hawkman raised his hand.

He could hear a female's voice coming from the room just ahead.

"I've got to take a break, ladies. When I come back, I'll bring you a bite to eat."

Quickly checking the room beside him, he motioned for Max and they slipped into a large linen closet in the nick of time. Keeping the door cracked a few inches they observed a woman, dressed in white with a ski mask over her head, step from the room.

Once in the hallway, she yanked off the hood and ran her fingers through long black hair that tumbled down her back. She wiped an arm across her face and ambled off in the opposite direction.

Hawkman frowned. Even though he didn't get a glimpse of the woman's face, she resembled Elaine Chen, Dr. Crowley's assistant.

Once she disappeared from sight, the two men eased out of the closet and approached the room. Standing on each side of the entrance, Hawkman reached down, took hold of the knob and eased open the door. He stepped over the threshold with his gun poised. Max followed.

The three ladies stared at them wide-eyed. Hawkman put his finger to his lips. Jennifer immediately pointed to the monitor hanging above the door. Max glanced up, took off his hat and hung it over the lens.

Hawkman then went to Jennifer's bedside. "There's also an intercom somewhere in this room," she whispered, as he wiped off the tears sliding down her cheeks.

He leaned close to her ear, kissed her cheek and whispered. "How the hell are you tied to this bed?"

She pointed underneath. "Like a seat belt." He reached under and released the buckle, then pulled the Buck knife from his boot and slashed the ankle ties.

When she attempted to rise, he gently pushed her down. "Stay put for now."

Max did the same with Carmen and she raised her arms, grabbed him around the neck in a hug, tears flowing down her cheeks. "Uncle Max," she said in a low husky voice. "I thought we were going to die."

He kissed her forehead and put a finger against her lips. "Don't move," he whispered. "We still have some things to take care of."

Hawkman hurried over to Destiny. Soft sobs wracked her body as he unfastened the bindings and released her feet. "Jesse and Amanda are going to be two happy people to see you again," he said softly.

She nodded and took a deep breath. "Thank you," she said between sniffles.

Hawkman slipped his rifle under the covers next to Jennifer. "Just in case you need it."

Max put his firearm on Carmen's cot and covered it with the sheet. Then the two men pulled their handguns from their holsters and positioned themselves against the wall at the back side of the door.

Five minutes lapsed before the hooded nurse walked in backwards, a tray loaded with covered dishes in her hand. She held the door open with her butt as she spouted instructions to the person accompanying her. "Hurry up, we don't have much time."

A masked man, also with a tray of food, scurried past her and turned toward Destiny's bed. The woman closed the door with her foot and headed toward Jennifer.

Max stepped up behind the man pushing his gun into his ribs. "Don't make a sound or you're dead meat," he whispered.

The nurse whirled around and stared into the barrel of Hawkman's .45.

He put his finger to his lips and pointed to the floor.

She slowly knelt, never taking her eyes off the gun and set the tray down. Hawkman motioned for Jennifer to get up and take the rifle he'd put next to her earlier. When she'd stepped aside, he tied the nurse's hands behind her, then motioned toward the bed. She crawled in and Hawkman placed the binding over her chest, then reached under the bed and locked them tightly. After securing her feet, he ripped off a piece of the sheet and started to tie it around her mouth. But then, he straightened, and yanked off her hood. Long black hair cascaded over Elaine Chen's shoulders as she looked up at him with wide brown eyes glistening with fear.

Hawkman glared at her as he leaned over and tied the gag around her mouth.

Max had secured his captive into Destiny's bed, then glanced at Hawkman and mouthed. "You know her?"

He nodded.

Max motioned for Carmen to get out of her bed and bring the gun. They all headed toward the entry. Hawkman raised his hand, opened the door a crack, then quickly shoved the women behind it.

"Someone's coming. They must have discovered the blank screen on their video monitor."

He and Max had no more flattened their backs against the wall when the door flew open and two hooded men, carrying assault rifles, dashed inside.

CHAPTER THIRTY-THREE

Hawkman leaped forward, swung his arm around one of the men's necks and held him in a crunching hold until it blocked off his air. When the man dropped to his knees, Hawkman grabbed his assault rifle and shoved the hefty body to the floor. Putting his booted foot on the enemy's neck, he pointed the gun at his head. "Don't move."

At the same time, Max whirled the other man around by his shoulder, slammed a punch to his jaw, then kicked him in the groin. The man went down so hard and fast, it was doubtful he knew what happened. Grabbing the gun from the rogue's hand, Max stepped back and blew on his knuckles.

Hawkman tied his prisoner's wrists with his last short rope. He glanced at Max who shook his head as he lashed the hands of his downed opponent. Hawkman yanked off the guy's hood, turned him over and crammed it into his mouth. He then motioned for Max to guard him while he crossed the room and pulled down the long drape that hid the windows. Using his buck knife, he slashed the heavy material into several long pieces. He tossed Max a couple of the strips. They finished tying and gagging the men, then pulled their bodies to the side of the room out of view of the doorway.

Since Hawkman and Max had given the women their firearms they took the guards' assault rifles. They found extra clips on the prisoners and slid them into their own jacket pouches.

Hawkman cocked his head and pointed toward the ceiling. The familiar rotary sound of a helicopter echoed in the distance. Again, he positioned the women behind the door and whispered into Jennifer's ear. "Use the rifle, if you have to."

Nodding, and with fear in her eyes, she stuffed the extra cartridges into her jeans pockets.

Hawkman planted a kiss on her forehead and gave her a quick hug, then reached over and gripped Destiny's shoulder. He could feel the girl's trembling body under his grasp. "It'll soon be over," he murmured.

Max tapped the gun Carmen held and also handed her extra ammunition. "Take anyone out that comes at you gals."

"Okay," she said, in a low shaky voice.

Hawkman glanced at Max. "Does she know how to use that?"

"Like a pro. Taught her myself."

The two men moved to the door and cautiously opened it a few inches. Finding the hallway clear, they slipped out of the room.

Still aware of the intercom, Jennifer motioned for Carmen to stay put as she moved across to the other side of the door. She crouched down, resting the rifle on her knee. Eyeing the bound prisoners, she wondered what they were thinking. Were they as frightened as she'd been, lying there and not being able to move? At least she hadn't been gagged with her hands tied behind her back. That must really make a person feel helpless.

Staring at the nurse, Jennifer knew Hawkman had recognized her when he pulled off the woman's hood. She didn't remember his talking about an Asian girl, but that didn't mean anything. There were a lot of things he didn't tell her during the run of a case. She'd find out later.

Suddenly, the loud noise of a helicopter close overhead vibrated the walls and made the windows rattle. Jennifer stood and glanced at the other two women. They lifted their gaze toward the ceiling.

Outside, the seven men from the bingo hall had gagged, tied and bound the captured guards to tree trunks in the heavily wooded area around the property. Then once they heard Hawkman's signal, had made their way toward the house, where each pair took a position on securing the exit doors. Argy and Frank slashed the tires on the red sports car parked in front.

Inside, with backs against the wall and guns poised, Hawkman and Max crept down the long hallway toward the front of the house. The aroma of food twirled around their noses, making them realize they hadn't eaten in hours.

The door to the kitchen stood open. The sound of humming and the rattling of pans came from within. Hawkman wondered how many people had been hired for this operation. So far he'd counted twelve: eight guards outside and four on the inside. Now a cook and possibly a helper.

They advanced toward the kitchen. When they reached the door, Hawkman motioned for Max to stay put and he'd go to the other side. But just as he moved across the open doorway, the cook glanced up, stopped humming, and dropped his spatula on the stove with a clatter. Hawkman turned and stepped toward the man, pointing the assault rifle at his belly. Max followed, closing the door behind him, then headed toward the rear of the room, searching behind each cabinet.

The cook's face lost its red flush from being over the heated stove and his eyes glistened with terror. After wiping his hands down his white apron, he raised them above his head and backed up.

"Stay still and keep calm, then no one will get hurt." Hawkman said in a low voice. "Who else works in here?"

"Me only," he said, in a quivering voice. "I cook for everyone. Guards come and get food. I no have any help."

About that time, a young woman in her early twenties, carrying a load of white folded towels with an Uzi hanging from a strap off her shoulder, strolled out of a small room at the back of the kitchen. When she saw Hawkman, she dropped the laundry and went for the weapon.

Max stepped up behind the girl and jabbed his rifle into

her back. "I wouldn't do anything stupid." He reached around and took the Uzi from her hands.

Her mouth screwed in disgust, she raised her arms. Max took a quick peek into the laundry room, then shoved her forward toward the cook.

The heavy set man's expression turned even more grim. "My daughter, she come every week to wash. Please, no hurt us."

"Any more of your family here?" Max asked the young woman.

She shook her head. "Only me and Papa."

"We'll talk to you later. Right now I want you out of here," Hawkman said. "Max, who's out back?"

"Teley."

"Have him take care of them."

Max guided the cook and his daughter to the back exit. He reached around the girl and opened the latch only to be met with a gun barrel aimed at his head. He raised his hand. "It's me, Teley. Get that thing out of my face." He pushed the prisoners outside. "Tie and gag these two. Keep them out of harm's way."

Teley nodded,

Hawkman flipped off the light switch. Then the two men slipped out of the kitchen. Keeping close to the wall, they crept down the hallway toward another room where they could hear loud but muffled conversation. A glow radiated from around the partially closed door.

As they got closer, Hawkman recognized the louder voice as the one that had made the threatening call to Jennifer. He tightened his hold on the gun and felt his neck muscles ripple.

The sound of the aircraft grew louder and would soon be directly overhead. Suddenly, the door flew open and a shaft of light shot through the darkness.

"Where the hell is everyone?" one of the men shouted. "I hear the helicopter. They should have the women ready to go by now."

Hawkman moved quickly into the shadows and crouched down behind a short wall that formed the foyer leading to the front door. Max promptly stepped inside a doorway that appeared to be a formal dining room.

Roland Alexander stood on the threshold, staring down the hall. "It's too damn quiet. And look." He pointed toward the kitchen. "It's always lit up in there, but now it's dark." He curled a hand around his mouth. "Hey, Boris. Got any food ready?" When he received no response, he whirled around and spoke into the room. "There's something wrong. I'm gettin' the hell outta here."

Hawkman brought the rifle to his chest and waited. Roland turned and grabbed a jacket from the back of a chair, then moved toward the door. The older Alexander stepped into view and grabbed his son's arm.

"No, you're stayin' here. Your pay includes taking a risk or two. We have to see to it that those women are loaded aboard that copter and on their way."

"There ain't a guard in sight out there. And listen." He cocked his head and pointed toward the ceiling. "That aircraft is just hoverin' up there. How come he hasn't set down?"

Mr. Alexander cuffed Roland on the arm. "We better go find out."

The son glanced over his dad's shoulder. "Where's Tony?"

"He's in the can," he said, hooking his thumb toward the back of the room. "We don't need him right now."

"Tony, meet us in the hostage's room," Roland called.

"Will do," came the response.

Roland and his dad each picked up an assault rifle off the couch and headed down the hallway.

CHAPTER THIRTY-FOUR

Hawkman didn't like the idea of jumping in front of the Alexanders while they toted those semi-automatic rifles. They hardly had to aim those buggers and he could end up dead or wounded.

He hunched back down in his hiding place and decided to let the two men go by and come at them from behind. But then he'd have to worry about Tony who might also be carrying a gun.

If they were headed to check on the girls, he and Max had to intercept them. His partner must have had the same idea as he hadn't stepped out of the dining room. When they'd worked together years ago, they'd developed the uncanny ability to almost read each other's minds. Looked like things hadn't changed much.

Roland and his dad hurried by the foyer without even glancing in his direction. Easing out of the shadows, Hawkman stayed close to the wall as he followed the two men. Across the hallway, Max stepped out of his hiding place and headed down the opposite side. Each kept a wary eye on the living room.

The helicopter's noise resonated loudly and Roland yelled as he pointed his rifle at the ceiling. "Why hasn't that damn bird landed?"

"Beats me," said his dad. Both men broke into a trot, passed the hostage room, and scurried toward the doorway leading to the garage.

Jennifer had left the door open a couple of inches so she

could keep an eye on the hallway. Her stomach leaped when she heard shouting, then saw Roland and his dad run past the room carrying guns. Were they behind this scheme? Where were Hawkman and Max? Her heart skipped a beat. Had they been captured? Then with a sigh of relief she spotted them trailing behind the Alexanders. Wiping a hand across her face, she took a deep breath to regain her composure and quickly cast a glance at the prisoners. None had moved and still appeared securely bound.

The constant noise of the aircraft overhead made her ears ring. The thought of its purpose sent a chill over her body. She gnawed her lip, thinking about seeing Mr. Alexander. What would he have to gain by kidnapping women? Roland and Tony would certainly do it for the money. Something about this picture didn't fit. She'd be glad when it all ended so she could get some answers. But right now they were still in grave danger and she mustn't let her guard down. She glanced at Carmen and Destiny, giving them a faint smile of encouragement.

Hawkman and Max hung back, knowing that Roland and his dad were about to get the surprise of their lives when they opened that door. The man and his son stopped in their tracks as they were met by Elvis' and Ralph's gun barrels aimed at their guts.

"I knew I should have got the hell outta here," Roland muttered as Ralph snatched his gun.

"Get your hands up," Elvis commanded.

Mr. Alexander took a step backwards, but Elvis rushed forward. Using the barrel of his gun, he knocked the rifle from the older man's hands, then aimed his weapon at the senior's belly.

"Don't try anything cute," Elvis said, his glare flashing with contempt. "I wouldn't like to splatter an old guy, but I will if you force me."

Mr. Alexander slowly raised his hands above his head.

Suddenly, shots rang out from the hostage room. Hawkman

and Max turned on their heels and raced toward the area. When they charged into the room, they found Tony sprawled on the floor, blood oozing from holes in his chest, his assault rifle still in his hand. Jennifer and Carmen stood with their weapons pointed at the fallen man.

Max kicked the gun out of reach, then knelt down and put his fingers on Ricardo's neck. After a few moments, he glanced up and shook his head. "He's dead."

The two women lowered their weapons.

"What happened?" Hawkman asked.

"He dashed into the room, then turned and spotted us," Carmen said, her voice shaking. "He raised his gun into firing position. We weren't about to chance being mowed down, so we fired first."

"How many more are out there?" Jennifer muttered.

Hawkman put his arm around her shoulder. "They're all taken care of, except for the helicopter gang. My cell phone's doesn't work in these hills, so I want you to go to the kitchen where I saw a phone. Call Detective Williams and get him out here."

She nodded. "I'm on my way."

"Carmen, can you guard these prisoners okay?"

Her eyes narrowed. "No problem."

He motioned for Max and they dashed out of the room and headed for the garage. Hawkman quickly plugged in the lights that lit up the landing pad. Then he and Max helped Elvis and Ralph pull the two restrained Alexanders into the garage out of sight.

While the helicopter maneuvered its way down, the four men stepped out and stood in full view on the ground with their guns across their chests. They figured the crew wouldn't recognize whoever guarded this place.

When the aircraft finally settled on the roof and the rotors stopped whirling, the hatch opened and two men stepped out. "What the hell took you so long turning on those lights?" the pilot yelled.

"Had some trouble with the circuit breakers. They kept popping off. Finally got it working," Hawkman answered.

"We're running late. Need to get the cargo loaded as quickly as possible," he said, climbing down the ladder alongside the garage. "Hope you've got us something to eat."

"How many of you?" Hawkman asked, eyeing the cockpit.

"Just me and Jack, my co-pilot," he said, moving aside to let his partner descend. "They told us we'd have three women and a helper to bring back, so we had to come light."

"Very good," Hawkman said, bringing his gun down and aiming at the two. Max, Elvis and Ralph closed ranks with their firearms.

"What the hell," the pilot said, glaring at the armed men encircling him and his companion.

Max stepped forward and patted them down to make sure they carried no weapons. The pilot's eyes popped in fear. "What the shit's going on?"

"This operation has just ended," Max said. "Gonna be a long time before you carry any more *cargo*."

About that time, sirens screamed in the background and flashing lights sent eerie streaks through the trees as several police cars surrounded the area. Uniformed men fanned through the wooded areas around the house, and brought forth gagged and tied prisoners from all directions.

Detective Williams hurried toward Hawkman and Max with a couple of officers who took the pilot and co-pilot away. He glanced up at the roof. "Hmm, wonder who owns that neat little machine? Sure would be a nice little asset to my department."

Hawkman laughed. "In your dreams. That thing will sit in a hanger for a year until the trial."

The detective nodded. "You're probably right." Williams shrugged. "Okay, where do you have the women stowed? When I heard Jennifer's voice come over the line I thought I was dreaming."

"Inside," Hawkman said, hooking a thumb toward the house. "They're guarding more prisoners."

Williams gave him a puzzled look. "There's more?" He scratched his head. "You two took all these guys by yourself?"

"No, we had a lot of help," Max said. "Let me introduce you to a couple of great guys." He extended his arm, but Elvis and Ralph had disappeared. "Where the hell did they go?"

"Maybe they've gone to check on the girls," Hawkman said, strolling toward the door. Then he turned and pointed at the garage. "You'll find two of the ringleaders tied up in there."

"And who might they be?" the detective asked, staring at the building.

"Alexander senior and his son, Roland. You'll need the coroner for Ricardo. He's inside the house."

"How'd that happen?"

"The women shot him. He charged into the room where they'd been held. Guess he got quite a surprise when he found a couple of his comrades tied up on the cots instead of the girls."

The detective frowned. "I don't follow you."

Hawkman sighed. "It's a long story and I'll fill you in later. But the women were drugged and bound to their beds. I want Carmen, Destiny and Jennifer examined thoroughly at the hospital to check the effects of the drugs and make sure they weren't abused."

Hawkman, Max and the detective entered the hostage room. The women glanced up and grinned with relief.

"Did Elvis and Ralph come by here," Hawkman asked.

"Yes," Jennifer said. "Elvis told us we looked beautiful and that he loved us. He left throwing kisses."

Hawkman chuckled. "Tonight I agree with him."

"It's all over, isn't it?"

He nodded and took Jennifer into his arms.

"Thank God," Carmen said, grasping her uncle's hand and collapsing onto the chair by the door.

"Mr. Casey, how can I ever thank you for coming to our rescue?" Destiny asked through tears. "I never thought I'd see my dad and little girl again."

Hawkman reached around Jennifer and pulled her into his

hug. "No need to thank me. Amanda, Jesse and Rochester have been very distraught. We had to find you."

Meanwhile, Detective Williams stepped across Tony's body and proceeded to the bedside of the bound woman. He stared at the tears rolling down her cheeks. "Well, well, who have we here? None other than Dr. Crowley's office assistant, Ms. Elaine Chen. No wonder Hawkman and I made you nervous when we visited the doctor's office." He reached down and untied the gag around her mouth. "It's too late for tears."

Her body shook with sobs as he tugged at the straps over her shoulders. When they didn't loosen, he followed the band over the side of the bed with his hand, then glanced underneath. "Quite a contraption and very escape proof." He flipped the buckle, cut the ankle binding with his pocket knife, then helped her to a standing position. "We'll leave your wrists bound until I get an officer up here with another set of cuffs. We've about run out."

Williams then crossed over to the other bed and removed that prisoner's gag. The man glared at him with hate. "Think we'll just leave you confined until more policemen arrive."

CHAPTER THIRTY-FIVE

Soon after the coroner left, the prisoners were hauled away in the police van, except for Elaine Chen. They drove her separately in one of the patrol cars along with the cook and his daughter. The ambulance had taken the three women to the local hospital for a thorough check up. The complete area had been cordoned off with yellow tape and the Mobile Crime Unit truck would remain for some time. Hawkman, Max and Detective Williams stood under the front porch light.

Williams folded his arms across his chest. "Okay, where's all this help you guys said you had? None of us saw any extra men guarding this place when we arrived. Yet, on each side of this house, my officers found these thugs tied to tree trunks deep in the woods. I think you're pulling my leg. Looks like you and Max did this job on your own."

Hawkman shrugged. "What can I say, other than we did have help. I have a feeling those guys didn't want any publicity."

"So you're not going to tell me who they are?"

"Nope," Hawkman said, shaking his head.

Max stood silently with what appeared to be a grin tickling the corners of his mouth.

Williams glanced at him. "And what are you smiling about?"

Max raised his brows in a surprised look and hooked a thumb to his chest. "Who, me? Smiling?"

Williams threw up his hands in defeat. "I give up. I'm going back to the station. We have to get this bunch booked. It will take awhile, so I won't be interrogating anyone for a day or two. I'll let you guys know so you can sit in."

"Sounds fine," Hawkman said. "Right now I'm going to the hospital to see Jennifer, then out to Jesse's."

The detective checked his watch. "Don't you think it's a little late to go see Wilson? It's way after midnight."

"He won't mind."

The men walked down the gravel driveway to the street, stepped over the yellow tape and headed for their vehicles. "Oh, by the way," Hawkman called to Detective Williams. "How long will you need to keep Jennifer's van?"

"Not more than a couple of days. I'll get the lab crew on it right away. In fact, they might be working on it tonight. Give me a call tomorrow."

Hawkman gave him a salute as he and Max climbed into the 4X4.

He put his hand into his pocket, then held out an open palm toward Max. "I need the keys, buddy."

"That's right. I drove this baby last. Nice vehicle," he laughed, dropping them into his hand.

Hawkman felt the weight of the last few hours lifting from his shoulders by the time he pulled in front of Max's apartment. "Thanks, pal. This couldn't have come to a happy ending without you."

Max waved him off. "Felt like old times. Let's do it again."

"I'll pick you up about five this evening. We better go to bingo and thank those volunteers."

Throwing back his head, Max let out a belly laugh. "Those guys are something else. I'll be ready. Think I'll go in now and call my brother. Nice to have good news for a change." He waved and trotted toward his flat.

Hawkman did a U-turn and headed for the hospital. The parking lot had plenty of spaces at this early morning hour, so he had no problem finding a spot close to the door. He hurried inside and went straight to the information desk to find out Jennifer's room. He rode the elevator to the third floor, found the doctor in charge, spoke with him for several minutes, then went to find his wife.

The door stood open with a nurse just leaving. He strolled in to find Jennifer, Carmen and Destiny sharing the same room as he was sure they'd requested. Smiling, he went to Jennifer's bed and pulled the curtain around for some privacy. He took her hand in both of his. "Hello, sweetheart. How's it going?"

She patted his arm and her hazel eyes glistened. "It's so good to be out of that hell-hole. We're so happy to be safe, thanks to you and Max."

"Don't forget the guys at the bingo hall. We couldn't have done it without them."

"I told you they were a bunch of wonderful men."

"Yes, I agree. They went well beyond the call of duty."

"I know you're concerned about what happened to us while we were in confinement. I spoke with Carmen and Destiny about their treatment, since they were prisoners for a much longer time. They were never sexually abused or touched by any of the men except for walking purposes. Elaine, aka Helen, was the person who escorted them to the bathroom for their personal needs. And that turned out to be true with me, too."

He squeezed her fingers. "That's a relief."

"Do you have any idea who the main players are in this deadly game?" she asked, frowning.

"No, and we'll probably never know. I doubt that even Alexander could name them, as it appears that all his orders came by way of phone or messenger. He hired Roland and Ricardo to kidnap the girls. However, we are aware of a group of wealthy foreign men working a world wide ring for hiring thugs to find beautiful women to act as sex slaves. I'm told the pay is quite lucrative."

She let out an audible sigh. "I can't understand Mr. Alexander getting into that type of thing. I thought he had plenty of money."

Hawkman shook his head. "Well, he did at one time, but I discovered he lost it all in the stock market."

Jennifer shivered. "So the helicopter would have whisked us away to God knows where?"

Hawkman pulled her into his arms. "I would have found you even if I had to travel to the ends of the earth."

She reached up and kissed him on the mouth. "I love you."

He held her close for several moments, then took a deep breath. "I'm going to leave so you can get some rest. The doctor said all of you ladies were in excellent health. Carmen and Destiny are free of drugs with no obvious aftereffects and your body checked out clear."

"Can we go home tomorrow?"

"Yes. I'll be here to pick you up in the morning."

Before he left the room, he called to Destiny. "I'm going out to see your dad right now. So be ready for a great reunion in a few hours."

She smiled. "Thank you. Tell him I love them."

Hawkman nodded. "Carmen, Max planned to call your father tonight. I'm sure they'll all be here."

"I can hardly wait to get home," she said, waving, a big grin on her face.

Hawkman left the hospital with a light heart. He could hardly wait to get to Jesse's place. When he rolled up in front of the farm house, the porch light glowed revealing Rochester in his same spot. When he climbed out of the 4X4, the hound raised up on his haunches and let out a mournful howl. Hopping onto the front porch, Hawkman reached down and scratched the him between the ears. "You're going to be one happy dog tomorrow."

He knocked softly and after a few seconds heard the cane thumping across the wooden floor.

When Jesse opened the door and saw Hawkman, his face registered fear. "What's you doin' here in the middle of the night?" he said, his voice cracking.

"We found Destiny, Jesse. She's alive and well. They have her in the hospital, running some precautionary checks. But she's just fine. She told me to tell you she loves you and Amanda and can hardly wait to get home. You can pick her up in the morning.

Tears welled in the old man's eyes. He dropped his cane and grabbed Hawkman in a bear hug. "God bless you, man. God bless you!" he sobbed.

Hawkman held Jesse tightly and realized tears were streaming down his own cheeks.

THE END